"If you knew me a little better, you'd know that I'm hardly ever disappointed."

"What if I disappoint you?" he asked.

He was going to kiss her. She could feel it in his touch and hear it in the lilt of his voice, and though she wanted it, there was a nagging voice in the back of her head that kept telling her how stupid it would be to let him. If he kissed her, the rules of their game would change. Their roles would be compromised. Her job would be compromised. Heck, even his future could be jeopardized.

"You won't," she said, as his lips grew nearer, so close that she shut her eyes and readied herself to feel his lips press against hers. "And we...can't," she said, nearly breathless.

But he didn't stop. And she didn't pull away.

Acknowledgments

This series wouldn't have been possible without a great team of people, including my agents and editors at Harlequin—thank you for all your hard work.

Also, thank you to Suzanne Miller and the crew at Dunrovin Ranch in Lolo, Montana. Suzanne is the inspiration behind one of my favorite characters in this series, the fantastic Eloise Fitzgerald. Just like Eloise, she always greets you with a warm smile and an open heart.

I'm proud to say that all proceeds from the events in honor of this series shall go to the Missoula, Montana, Girls Using Their Strengths (GUTS!) program. This program empowers and promotes leadership in girls aged nine to eighteen. It is my belief that we must support and help empower young women so someday they can run the world.

MS. DEMEANOR

DANICA WINTERS

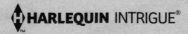

To Mac.

No matter what comes our way,
we will always move our story forward.

ISBN-13: 978-1-335-72141-9

Ms. Demeanor

Copyright © 2017 by Danica Winters

Please Recycle — This Product is Recyclable

Recycling programs
for this product may
not exist in your area.

Printed in U.S.A.

HARLEQUIN®
www.Harlequin.com

Danica Winters is a multiple award-winning, bestselling author who writes books that grip readers with their ability to drive emotion through suspense and occasionally a touch of magic. When she's not working, she can be found in the wilds of Montana, testing her patience while she tries to hone her skills at various crafts—quilting, pottery and painting are not her areas of expertise. She believes the cup is neither half-full nor half-empty, but it better be filled with wine. Visit her website at danicawinters.net.

Visit the Author Profile page at Harlequin.com.

CAST OF CHARACTERS

Rainier Fitzgerald—One heck of a bad boy and ultimate charmer of Mystery, Montana. After returning to his family's ranch, the last thing he expected was to find himself knee-deep in another scandal.

Laura Blade—As Rainier's parole officer and one of his few allies, she quickly realizes she is falling for the man she's been charged with helping. In order to truly help the handsome Fitzgerald, she must go toe-to-toe with her hard-edged father and hope that he can give them the answers they need.

Eloise Fitzgerald—Foster mother and caregiver not only to the people in her life, but to the animals as well. She is the head matriarch of the Fitzgerald clan—but even she has secrets.

Merle Fitzgerald—The patriarch of the Fitzgerald clan and foster father to four sons. With a heart as big as his ranch, he has an amazing capacity for understanding and forgiveness—even for those who don't believe they are deserving.

Dennis Blade—Laura's no-nonsense father and a high-powered attorney. He always expects the worst in people, even Laura.

William Poe—A shady county tax appraiser who thinks everyone and everything belongs to him—even the women of Mystery, Montana. When his family's history crosses paths with that of the Fitzgeralds, he will use it to try to destroy everything they hold dear.

Wyatt Fitzgerald—Waylon's brother and the local sheriff's deputy who quickly finds himself neck-deep in an investigation that calls into question not only his investigative skills, but a whole slew of his family's history.

Paul Poe—William Poe's father, who had just about as many secrets as his son—secrets that may threaten the ranch and all those who call it home.

Chapter One

There was nothing quite like the rush he'd felt when he had tried to kill his father. It had been like a charge running through Rainier Fitzgerald, shooting up from his toes straight through his body and escaping in one ill-advised and perfectly placed punch. One hit, one single punch had cost him more than three years of his life, thousands of dollars and nearly all his relationships.

There were times he wished he had really killed his biological father. Just a little bit harder or just a few more punches and he could've watched the life slip from the man's body. If he had died, maybe then Rainier could've felt guilty about what he had done to him; as it was, the only regret he held was that he hadn't punched him sooner.

The prison's chain-link gate vibrated; metal ground against metal and made an ear-piercing squeal as the gate opened. Rainier had been dreaming about this day, the day of his release, since the moment he'd entered this hellhole.

He took in a deep breath. The cold air carried the heavy and earthy scent of concrete, dirt and broken dreams, but he didn't care—for the first time in years, he was free.

The only hint it was nearly Christmas was the thick layer of snow on the ground and the black sedan in the parking lot complete with a set of felt reindeer antlers poking out of its passenger's- and driver's-side windows.

They looked ridiculous, but a hoarse chuckle escaped him, the sound so foreign that it caught him off guard.

In the corner of its windshield, the car had a parking decal for the Montana State Prison. Whoever it belonged to must work at this place, or was here enough that it was deemed necessary for them to have quick access—which made the Christmas fare seem even more asinine and somewhat obscene. It was as if the owner celebrated the fact that they could enjoy their freedom, even if it meant buying cheesy holiday decorations and displaying them from their cars for the inmates to see—and hate them for.

He looked around the parking lot, hoping to see Wyatt in one of their father's ranch trucks or maybe his patrol vehicle. Rainier smirked as he considered the irony of being picked up from prison in a squad car. Only in his life would something so ridiculous be possible.

But the only truck was an old beat-up Dodge at the far end of the parking lot. The pickup was empty and a film of ice covered the windshield as if it had been parked there for days.

His brother had left him in the lurch. He shouldn't have been surprised, but a promise was a promise.

Rainier sighed, rubbing his hands together as he tried to stave off the cold; though, if someone would have asked, it wasn't the chill of winter that caused him to shiver but rather the icy reception from his family.

On the other hand, he could hardly blame his brother for not coming here to pick him up after everything he'd put the family through. It was the same reason he hadn't asked his mother to come get him—he hated her seeing him in this kind of place. All she'd ever done was take care of him and shower him with love, and yet he repaid her by being sent to a place where meals were given on a tray and people told him what time he could take a shower. In some ways, he felt like the bastard child he'd always been—thrown into foster care and finally picked up by the Fitzgeralds. They'd always made him feel like one of them, just another one of the adopted sons. Yet now here he was, alone and adrift again.

The door to the black sedan opened, the reindeer

antler on the driver's-side door jiggling wildly, like a hand waving him down, as a woman stepped out. To say she was beautiful was an understatement. No, she was far more than that. Her ashy-blond hair was pulled tight into a no-nonsense bun, a pair of tortoiseshell-framed glasses teetered on the top of her head and her legs were long, and he couldn't look away from the round contours of her luscious hips. She turned, bending over to get something out of her car, forcing him to stop midstep as her pencil skirt hugged the curves of her ass. His mouth watered as he stared at the diagonal lines her panties created as they pressed against the fabric.

Maybe he had been imprisoned too long, but she might just be the sexiest woman he'd ever seen. She was dignified, classy and clearly the kind of woman who wouldn't have a damn thing to do with him. She was a far cry from the type of women whose pictures decorated most inmates' cell walls within his unit, as most of the pictures had been ripped out of men's magazines.

She stood up and patted her jacket pocket, searching for something. He was pretty sure he saw her mouth form a collection of profanities, which seemed in direct opposition to the lines of her skirt and the straight-edged look on her face. It made him only want her that much more.

Yep, he had definitely been behind bars way too

long. He'd never have a chance at a girl like that, not being the man he was, but that didn't mean he wasn't the kind who wouldn't swing for the fences.

She reached into her purse, rifling through its contents as he made his way toward her.

"Can I help you, ma'am?" he asked. "You lose something?"

She jerked as though she hadn't noticed him. She lifted her hand, motioning for him to stop. "I'm fine. Just fine," she said, then cleared her throat as though she were trying to collect her nerves. In fact, from the way her eyes widened, she looked almost scared of him.

He should have anticipated that this was what his life was to become when he got out—people fearing him, the feral Fitzgerald.

"I'm sorry, I didn't mean to bother you. Just thought, ya know…" His voice came out hoarse and tattered, befitting the man he had become. He turned to walk away.

"Wait." The woman's heels clicked against the pavement behind him as she rushed to catch up.

He swiveled back, and for a split second he could have sworn her gaze had been locked on his ass—or it could just be wishful thinking.

"Yeah?" he asked, cocking a brow.

"You're Rainier Fitzgerald, correct?" She lifted a

phone he hadn't notice she'd been carrying, and was met with his mug shot from the day he'd been booked.

He stared at the picture. His green eyes looked nearly black. The only thing that gave away his fear over heading to jail was the slight quirk of his lip. He always looked like he was about to smile when he was nervous. Reaching up, he touched his lip and realized he was making the same face now— except, unlike in the photo, a new set of fine lines surrounded his mouth, thanks to his years of hard living.

"Is this you?" she asked, flipping the phone so she, too, could look at the picture.

"Did Wyatt send you to be my welcoming committee? If he did, I'm going to have to thank him." The words came out wrong, sounding far more crass than he had intended.

"Excuse me?" she asked. "I don't know what you're implying, Mr. Fitzgerald. And while I'm sure you would love a warm welcome, I'm far from being someone who is available or willing to supply you with such a thing. Plus, it might be in your best interest to steer clear of women who would be interested in *welcoming* you."

He hadn't been out of prison for five minutes and he was already in trouble with a woman and, in an upper-crust way, being told exactly where he could stuff his feelings for the opposite sex.

About right.

"Hey, I'm sorry for thinking maybe you were here to welcome me to the real world. I guess I just hoped, you being as beautiful as you are and all…"

It could have been the cold, but her cheeks seemed to take on a darker shade of pink as she readjusted her suit jacket and cleared her throat again. "Mr. Fitzgerald—"

"Call me Rainier."

"Let me guess, *Mr. Fitzgerald* is your father?" she asked, her tone laced with distaste, as though she had heard that failed line more than a time or two.

"Actually, I wasn't thinking that at all. No one calls my father that, either." He motioned toward his hot pink Hawaiian shirt the prison had given him, one he was sure they had gotten for pennies on the dollar at the nearest thrift shop. "Does it look like I'm the kind of guy who should be called *mister*?"

There it was, her elusive smile flickering over her features. He was breaking through her icy exterior.

"Mister or not, *Rainier*, you need to watch yourself. I'm your parole officer. The name's Laura Blade."

He instinctively glanced down at the packet of papers he'd been given on the inside. Now her cool attitude made all kinds of sense. Of course she was from the other side of the law. "I thought I was supposed to report to your office tomorrow?"

"Your brother is a friend of mine. He requested we meet and you hear the terms and conditions of your release as soon as possible."

"Are you kidding me? My brother sent you to meet me at the door? Did he really think I was going to find myself in trouble so fast that I needed you to come here and warn me to toe the line?"

She tapped at her phone as though she was texting. "Actually, I had other errands to attend to, as well. You are hardly the only parolee I get the pleasure of seeing. Plus I'm always there for my brothers in blue."

"I bet Wyatt laughed his ass off when he set this up. Is he going to leave me here to figure out my own way home, too?"

"You must think little of your brother." She waved him off as he opened his mouth to argue. "Don't worry, I offered to escort you. I need to perform a home visit, anyway, so I can make sure you will not find yourself returning to Montana's famous legal system."

"You mean infamous?" he said, snorting.

"It's hardly as infamous as you," she said, motioning for him to get into her car.

He stared at her. "Are you serious?"

"What do you mean?" she asked, swinging her around her finger.

"Are you really offering to take me—a convicted felon—on a road trip all the way to Mystery?"

"I'm not your father, so I think I'm safe driving you home," she said. "Now hurry up and get in. It's not getting any warmer out here." She walked around to her door and the reindeer antlers jiggled as she sat down. She continued to tap on her phone as she waited for him.

He stood still for a moment, staring at the blonde before he got in next to her. She had done her research about him, but that didn't mean he wasn't dangerous. When it came to her, he could think of several things that he wanted to do—most of which involved kissing her pink lips and hearing her moan his name.

Then again, he'd always been the kind of guy to want what he could never have.

Maybe this tightly wound woman was more like him than he'd assumed. Maybe she liked to live life on the wild side.

Chapter Two

Laura had always thought it was just some stupid saying, but it was true that no good deed went unpunished. She'd thought Wyatt's request to help his brother would be easy and quick, and yet it had turned into her sitting next to a far-too-handsome convict for one painfully long and awkward road trip.

She glanced over at Rainier. His hair was flecked with bits of auburn and copper, and when the sunshine struck it just right it almost glowed like precious metal. His eyes were the color of emerald sea glass, their hue dulled and muted by the many years he'd spent behind bars. She wondered if, with time, their color would brighten and energy and light would return.

Her palms were sweaty as she gripped the steering wheel. The Dunrovin Ranch wasn't that much farther. She tried to nonchalantly glance at the clock on the dashboard to get an idea of how much more time she would be trapped in the car, but she noticed Rainier watching her and so she reached over and flipped on the radio. An old country song by George Jones filled the space between them, telling of broken hearts and destroyed lives. It was a bit ironic—the two of them were far too much like the song, she being the keeper of a broken heart, and his life destroyed.

She slipped Rainier a smile, trying to hide her thoughts before he could read them upon her face. Maybe she had it all wrong, or at least backward— her life had been destroyed in just a matter of minutes, as well.

Maybe the song was really just about her.

The country singer's twang grated on her nerves and she flicked off the radio.

"Do I need to go back over the rules and conditions of your parole, or do you think you understand them?" Laura asked, pushing a wayward strand of hair back into the tight bun on her head.

Rainier answered with a chuckle and lifted the manila envelope for her to see. "Between this ream of paper, and instructions you've been going over for the last hour, I think I've got it."

"I just want to make sure you fully understand that at any point we can revoke your parole, and you can be sent back to prison. Under no circumstances are you to violate any of the conditions I've given you."

"All right, there will be no drinking in excess, no hanging out where drugs are distributed or taken. I shall not leave my geographic limits without written permission. I shall see you between the first and third of each month…" He looked over at her and gave her a sexy half smile, and she tried to diffuse her nervousness by shifting in her seat. "I will not violate any law," he continued. "I won't associate with people who have criminal records, will not possess firearms or any dangerous weapons, and…well, we know the rest."

"Just so long as you do." She tapped her fingers on the steering wheel.

It was going to be a long year, seeing him every month, if this was the way he made her feel simply by sitting next to her and smiling.

Long ago, she had sworn off relationships, as the only thing they had ever brought her was heartache, thirty pounds that had now collected solidly around her thighs and ass, and what she'd learned later was a raging case of crabs. Not that she ever told anyone she'd had crabs, but she could think of no better reason to call an unwavering hiatus on all things men than a hundred little bugs making her itch like a madwoman. Looking back, she realized they weren't half as annoying as the man who'd given them to her.

"Laura—"

"Call me Ms. Blade," she said, interrupting.

"Sorry. *Ms. Blade.*" He said her name as if it were as sharp as the object it implied. "I was just gonna ask how you got into the parole officer game."

The last thing she needed was to exchange pleasantries with her assigned parolee. It would send the wrong message if Rainier thought for one minute they were anything that resembled friends. He had been assigned to her by the state, and her one job was to make sure he didn't find himself back in trouble. It was her job to save him from himself, even if that meant drawing a hard line.

"Being a parole officer isn't a game, Mr. Fitzgerald." She could feel her butt clench. "I take my job very, very seriously."

"Very very," he teased. "I guess you do. I haven't heard anybody say that since high school."

Just like in high school, she wanted to reach over and punch him in his arm for his cheeky manner. Under a different set of circumstances, she could've lightened up and they could've been friends. But he was the one who had chosen to nearly kill a man. Now he would have to deal with the consequences— not that missing out on her friendship was really a consequence that he needed to worry about.

"I'm surprised you didn't get into more trouble in prison, with a mouth like that."

He laughed, tilting his head back with mirth. "If you think I have a mouth, you clearly haven't been a parole officer very long. What are you—like, thirty-two?"

Oh, they were so off on the wrong foot.

It was never okay for a man to guess a woman's age, especially if he was guessing too high. If he had said twenty-four, things may have gone more in his favor, but it was too late. He had fallen from her grace.

Thankfully, they ascended the hill that led to the ranch, and the tin roof of the Dunrovin barn came into view, letting him off the hook about erroring at her age.

It had been only about a week since she'd come to the ranch for their annual holiday party, the Yule Night festival, and it felt strange coming back again so soon. Yet even with all the drama that surrounded the place, a sense of calm came over her. She could almost imagine what it would be like to live there, walking through the spring pastures with her feet splashing in the mud, or her fingers touching the heads of the summer grasses that they would cut and bale for hay, or feeling the nibble of the crisp fall air while they moved the animals from their summer pastures.

She sucked in a long, deep breath, hoping that some of the ranch's clean air had somehow slipped into the car. She could smell the faint aroma of horses, hay and diesel from the tractors. It was a heady mix, beckoning memories of her childhood spent daydreaming about horses and ranch life while her father whiled away the hours at his law office.

"I bet you're glad to be home," she said.

He glanced out the window, and she could swear that his green eyes turned a shade darker as he looked at the ranch. It didn't make sense how she could love this place so much and he could seem so disconnected.

"I'm glad to be out of prison," he grumbled.

"That doesn't mean that you're glad to be here."

"Oh, I'm glad to be home, but you gotta understand that I ain't gonna be welcomed with open arms. I screwed everything up. My brothers were so pissed, by now they have to have convinced everyone that it would be best if I just hit the road and never came back."

"I doubt your parents feel like that."

"They didn't come visit me. Not once when I was behind bars. They made it real clear they think I'm nothing but trouble."

"If you feel like your return to the family is going to inhibit your success in staying out of trouble, perhaps I can help you get settled elsewhere."

He grimaced as though she had just sentenced him to solitary confinement. "Nah, I ain't gonna run away. I'm just going to have to face whatever is coming my way."

She wanted to reach over and grip his fingers and give them a reassuring squeeze, but instead she gripped the steering wheel harder. "No matter what, I've got your back. I'm your ally."

"Well, at least I got one," he said, the sexy smile returning.

She pulled to a stop, parking the car in the gravel lot, which was covered in patchy snow. The ranch carried the warmth and feeling of Christmas, with its strings of lights, poinsettias and an abundance of wreathes that hung from every post. It looked like something out of a Norman Rockwell painting, including the older woman who was standing on the porch of the main office looking out at them.

She recognized Ms. Eloise Fitzgerald from passing and the occasional hello, and as they unbuckled, Eloise smiled and waved. Yet it was the congenial, halfhearted wave of a near stranger and a far cry from what Laura would have expected a mother to give her son.

Rainier's features darkened as he looked at his mother, having noticed her chilly reception himself.

"Don't worry, she probably just doesn't see you or something," Laura said, trying to soften the blow for him.

She stepped out of the car, Rainier following suit.

Eloise shaded her eyes, casting shadows over her face as she looked toward them. Her mouth opened as she must have finally recognized Rainier when he stepped around the front of the car and made his way toward the office.

She smiled and her curved back straightened as she stood a bit taller. "Rainier, sunshine, is that really you?" Eloise asked, excitement fluttering through her words. "I can't believe it!" She rushed forward and threw her arms around her son's neck. "Your father and I didn't think you'd be here until tomorrow. Wyatt said…" Her words where muffled against Rainier's chest as she tightened her arms around him.

The reunion made a lump form in Laura's throat. Thank goodness it wasn't the chilly reception that he had expected and she thought had come to fruition.

In the history of hugs, this one may have been the longest, as tears collected in the corners of Eloise's eyes and slipped down her cheeks. "I'm so glad you're home," she repeated over and over.

Rainier gave his mother a kiss on the top of her head and finally she stepped back, releasing him from her grateful hold. For the first time since seeing her son, she seemed to notice Laura.

"Laura, I can't tell you how thankful I am in having you bring my boy back to us." She reached over and gave her hand a warm squeeze. "You have to come in. The girls and I just made a batch of cookies and there's fudge cooling on the counter."

Fudge and cookies. Laura pulled at the waistband of her skirt. This time of year, the pounds always seemed to jump onto her thighs at the mere nearness of fudge and cookies. In fact, if she closed her eyes and thought about it, she could almost feel herself expanding.

"I'd love to, but first I need to make sure that all will be well with you and your family regarding your son's parole." She tugged on the hem of her skirt, lowering it. "Is Rainier going to be staying with you and working here on the ranch? Is he welcome?"

Eloise gave her a disbelieving look. "Are you kidding, dear? Everyone is welcome at the ranch. My son made mistakes, and he's paid for them. I don't want things for him to be any harder than they already are. I would do anything for him."

Her admiration for Eloise grew. It wasn't every day that a convicted felon was treated with such kindness, even by family members or loved ones.

Laura looked over at Rainier as Eloise took them both by the hand and led them toward the main house and the waiting smorgasbord of sweets. He sent her a brilliant smile, his white teeth sparkling in the winter sun. He was so handsome; it was easy to see how someone could forgive him for his mistakes and trust him with their heart.

Chapter Three

The house was a flurry of motion. Gwen and Eloise were rushing around the kitchen, pulling together a meal reminiscent of the epicurean lifestyle of ancient Greece. Every countertop was filled to the edge with food. There was everything from cold cuts and cheese to spritz cookies and rosettes. His mouth watered. The food was a far cry from what had been ladled onto his tray in prison and the little packs of chips he bought at the commissary. Dang, it was good to be home.

His mother handed him a plate full of food, and another to Laura, as though she was just one of the gang and not someone with the ability to put him back in prison. He couldn't decide whether it was a part of his mother's plan that she overwhelm Laura with kindness in hopes it would keep him out of trouble, or if it was just his mother's way. Regardless, he loved her for it.

His adoptive father, Merle, walked into the kitchen while thumbing through a stack of mail. In all the excitement his mother must have forgotten to tell him that Rainier was home. When he finally looked up from the letters in his hands, a wave of recognition and pure joy overtook his face.

"Son, what are you doing here? I thought you didn't get out for another couple of days?" His father gave a questioning glance to his mother.

"Oh, dear, I'm sorry. I meant to come get you. I just wanted to make sure that Rainier and Laura were taken care of. I'm so sorry," she said, throwing her hands over her mouth. "I can't believe…"

"It's okay, Mother," Merle said, giving her a quick peck on the forehead before turning to Rainier. "How long have you been home?"

He shrugged. With all the activity and questions his mother had been throwing his way, he wasn't sure if he'd been home five minutes or five hours. He wasn't used to this kind of attention, as if the world revolved around him. He both despised and loved it, but it was almost too much.

Even though he'd said nothing, his father seemed to understand and gave an acknowledging tip of his head.

"We haven't touched your room, Rainier. It's waiting for you if you're tired. This week we can go get you some new clothes," his mother said, coming over and pinching the pink Hawaiian shirt between her fingers and pulling it as if she wished she could throw it away then and there. "And we can get you anything else you need to get on your feet, as well. Waylon, Christina and Winnie will be coming home later this week." She grinned with excitement. "It's just going to be so wonderful to have the entire family here to spend Christmas. And Laura, you'll have to come, too."

Laura gaped as she glanced from his mother to him, almost as though she was checking him to see what exactly her reaction should be to that unusual invitation. "I...er..."

"You are more than welcome, Laura," his father said, jumping in. "You don't have to answer us right away. I'm sure you've got your own family plans."

She looked a bit relieved, and it made Rainier's chest tighten as some part of him wished she had agreed to spend more time with him and his family. He took a deep breath as he tried to make sense of his body's reaction. He barely knew this woman, and their conversation had been limited mostly to business. Yet he couldn't deny there was something, a spark, between them. It was so strong he could have sworn he felt it in his fingertips.

Maybe it was just that she was the only person who had any real understanding of what his life had been like behind bars. She was his ally, and seemed to be the only one who could understand why he had changed.

"I… Y-you…" he stammered, trying to say something that would be as effectual as his father, but no words came.

Merle smiled. "Rainier and I are gonna head outside. I need to get to work on that broken spigot before the pump burns out." His father handed him a coat, and he shrugged it on.

He couldn't have been more relieved and thankful for his father's interference not just with the jacket, but with helping him to get out of the swirl of activity that made him feel so out of place.

Laura's face relaxed as she glanced over to him and gave an approving nod.

"If he's going to be home, you know we're gonna be putting him to work," the older man continued.

She gave a light laugh. "That's exactly what I was hoping for, Mr. Fitzgerald. If you don't mind, while you all are working, I'll take a quick look around, a brief home check."

"That's fine, but please call me Merle." His father frowned at the formal moniker.

"Thank you, *Merle*," Laura said.

"That's better," his father said. "Only Mother calls me Mr. Fitzgerald, and she only does that when I'm in deep trouble." He turned to Rainier. "Let's get going. We're burning daylight."

He followed his dad outside, and the moment the door opened and he breathed in the cold winter air, Rainier was thankful to be out of the kitchen. He loved his mother and the rest of his extended family, but he needed a minute just to be with himself in the quiet of life—an existence that wasn't framed by steel bars.

His father led him out to the tractor and, handing him the keys, motioned for him to take a seat. "Sometimes the best thing we can do when our world is a mess is bury ourselves in work in order to clear our minds. There are no prisons worse than the ones we impose upon ourselves."

The man was right. No matter how bad the nights had been when he'd been inside, the worst of them all had come when Rainier had thought about what he'd cost his family. There were so many things he wanted to say, but one in particular came to the front of his mind. "Thanks for everything, Dad."

It didn't seem like nearly enough, but emotions and expressing them had never been his strong suit. It was just so much easier to bottle everything up— although that was exactly the kind of attitude that had gotten him into trouble in the first place.

"Which spigot needs tending?" he asked, afraid of things taking another emotional turn. He'd had more than he could handle for one day.

His father's stoicism thankfully returned, his face

taking on the smooth and patient coolness that Rainier had always loved about the man. Since he'd left, however, his father's face had seemed to age. In fact, he noticed a new darkness in his eyes and it made a deep sadness move through him. Undoubtedly, he had played a role in those changes, and there was no going back or making things right. There was only moving forward.

"It's the one in the pasture. If you want to start digging, I'll grab the piping," Merle father said.

His father tracked through the snow toward the back of the house. Climbing up onto the tractor, Rainier could see a dark patch of grass and soot where the toolshed had once stood.

The tractor chugged to life and he moved the old beast toward the well as he thought about all the things his family had gone through when he'd been away, and what all else could have happened that his mother hadn't told him.

The earth was hard with the freeze as he set to digging up the piping around the frost-free spigot his family used for watering the animals throughout the year. The tractor's bucket broke through the top of the dirt, and as he dug deeper, the frozen soil turned into a muddy mess of gravel and clay as the water from the well spilled from the leaking pipes and saturated the ground. Water poured from the sides of the bucket as he moved the earth, piling it to one side.

It felt good to be working again, to be contributing to his family and the ranch. If he could work here for the rest of his life, he would die a happy man— he didn't want a job like Laura's, some nine to five.

He scraped out another bucketful of dirt from the hole. As he emptied it onto the pile, something white protruded from the sticky, brown earth. The object looked like a long stick, but its end was round and knobby.

An uneasiness rose up from his belly as he shut off the tractor, the bucket lowered midway. He stepped down from the machine and made his way across the sticky mud.

As he grew near, the thing lurched slightly, settling with the dirt around it. Based on the grooves and speckles on the surface, it was definitely a bone. He swallowed back the nerves that had tightened his throat as he reminded himself that, even though it was a bone, it was probably nothing—just some animal remains or detritus of days gone by.

He picked up the bone, scraping away the mud as he turned it in his hands. It was stained brown from the tannins in the dirt, the long shaft darker than the round ball of the joint. He wasn't absolutely sure, but it looked terrifyingly similar to a human femur. He laid the bone down near the base of the hill.

Turning back to the pile of dirt, he looked through it, hoping not to see another piece of bone. He scratched at the cold earth, the dirt and gravel tearing at his fingertips as he frantically searched for anything that could help him make sense of what he had found. His wet fingers grew icy as he worked away, then stopped abruptly when he touched something hard and even colder. His hand closed around something L-shaped and, as he pulled it from the mud, he gave a small, muffled cry. In his grip was a gun.

There was the clang of metal on metal as pipes hit the ground and bounced behind him. He turned to see his father and Laura looking at him. Merle gasped in shock.

Rainier dropped the muddy weapon, letting it fall to his feet as he looked at Laura's pale face.

"What are you doing with a gun, Rainier?" she asked, disgust and horror filling her voice as she stared at it, and at the bone lying beside it. "You— you haven't been out of prison for five hours and yet here you are, back to your old ways."

"I swear…it's not what you think," he argued, raising his dirty hands, palms up. "It… I didn't know it was a gun when I picked it up."

She shook her head. "You can take it up with the judge. In the meantime, you can kiss your parole goodbye."

Chapter Four

He couldn't go back to prison. For a moment, Rainier considered running, just grabbing one of the old ranch trucks and hitting the highway. Thanks to the many letters his mother had sent him when he'd been away, he'd learned all about the murder at the hands of his former sister-in-law Alli and her escape from persecution. It seemed that law enforcement in Montana was usually two steps behind. Then again, thanks to his own experiences, he wasn't sure he could rely on that to be completely true, or he would have never found his ass in prison.

"Laura—"

"Ms. Blade," Laura interrupted, as she typed something into her phone.

"My apologies, *Ms. Blade*," he said, careful to use the same sharp tone. "It's just that I don't… I can't go back to prison. That wasn't my gun. Hell, I didn't even know it was a gun until it was in my hand. You have to believe me, I never want to waste my time behind bars again."

She stared at him for a long moment, and from the set of her jaw and the look in her eyes, he could tell she was struggling to believe him. He had no idea what else to tell her. No doubt, as a parole officer, she would have learned by now that very few people in this world told the truth—and even fewer who were ex-cons.

He'd long ago given up the idealistic notion that anyone would take anything he had to say at face value ever again. The moment the judge's gavel hit the block and he'd been delivered the sentence, Rainier had known he'd forever wear a scarlet letter for his crimes. Part of that sentence would be always being thought of as less than and dishonorable—no matter how justified he felt in committing the crime.

"Can't we just look past this, Ms. Blade?" asked his father. Merle held his hands together almost as if he was silently praying that Laura would honor his request.

Rainier could've told him a long time ago that that kind of thing had a way of blowing back on a guy.

"Mr. Fitzgerald, I know your family's been through a lot in the last month, but that doesn't mean I can just ignore what's going on here." Laura frowned. "I made it very clear to your son that there were certain conditions associated with his parole—

conditions he absolutely could not violate. And yet here we are. I can only imagine the kind of trouble he would find himself in if I *wasn't* here."

"I can assure you that my son has always been a good man."

"Let me guess—he's *just misunderstood*?" Her lips puckered as she spat the words out like watermelon seeds.

"I'm not going to make any excuses for my son's behavior, but you have to know that he wouldn't intentionally find himself in trouble. Especially not like this."

Her gaze swung to Rainier and he nodded, hoping that she would listen to both of them.

"Ms. Blade, it's not like I'm asking for a second chance. I'm just asking for any chance at all." Rainier hated the note of pleading in his voice. He'd never been one to beg, but he'd never been given his freedom and then had it rescinded on the same day.

"The police are on their way." Laura pushed her phone into her back pocket. "I won't tell them about the gun in your hand and the remains at your feet, but you have to promise me that this was just a case of you being at the wrong place at the wrong time and nothing else."

A sense of relief washed over him, but faded away again as the piercing sound of sirens echoed in the distance. He looked in that direction, but in the bright afternoon light couldn't make out their source. Hopefully, his brother wasn't on duty. The last person he needed to see right now was Wyatt.

"Do you promise, Rainier?" Laura pressed.

"Of course," he said, trying to sound earnest.

"And you won't find yourself in any more trouble?" she continued.

"You're welcome to stick around and be my wingman as long as you like, Ms. Blade," Rainier said, giving her a cheeky smile he hoped would ease some of the tension between them.

The parole officer looked away, making him wonder if his smile had worked, after all.

"Son, it may not be a bad idea for you to go inside and get out of the spotlight," his father said, motioning toward the house.

On the drive back to the ranch, Rainier had told Laura he wasn't afraid and that he wouldn't run away from whatever life would bring him. But now, facing the possibility of seeing his brother after all this time, the urge was strong to tuck tail and run on back to the house. Heck, he could even pretend that when his brother questioned him about the remains and the gun that it was the first he was hearing about the findings. Wyatt would probably think nothing of it, and he certainly wouldn't jump to conclusions like he would if he arrived and Rainier was standing by disarticulated remains.

His brother had always been like that with him—always thinking the worst. Rainier couldn't blame him for the trouble he himself got into; he'd always been a little bit of a rebel and the family's black sheep. But his brother's condescending attitude certainly didn't help. It was like every time he screwed up, Wyatt was there to let him know he had seen it coming.

Once, when they had been young boys, their parents had sent them out to collect eggs from the henhouse. Gathering eggs soon turned into Rainier picking up rocks and pitching them to see who could throw the farthest. Colter and Waylon had joined right in, using different size rocks and different throwing techniques until they had found the one that suited them best. But not Wyatt. Wyatt had stood to the side and kept warning them about how much trouble they were going to get into if their parents found them, or if something went wrong.

Of course, the other three didn't listen, and it wasn't five minutes before Rainier pitched the perfect pebble straight into the back window of their father's old Jeep. If he closed his eyes, he was sure he could still hear the crackling sound of the splintering glass, almost like someone stepping on the thin crust of ice on a lake.

Breaking that window had been his first lesson in keeping Wyatt out of his affairs and away from anything fun, as well as how much work it took to raise two hundred dollars to pay for a new window. His father had been understandably angry at the time, but just like now, he'd seemed to understand that sometimes bad things happened. A person could go about living his life between the lines, or as Merle put it, "living between the mustard and the mayonnaise," but even then couldn't avoid trouble. Or maybe Rainier wasn't really the kind who avoided it; maybe he was just as bad and destructive as people expected him to be.

"Rainier, are you listening?" asked Laura.

He hadn't heard a single thing she said.

"Sorry, what did you say?" he asked, blinking away images of him and his brothers playing around the ranch and causing trouble when they were younger. What he would give to go back to those days, when they'd all still got along and had truly lived for each other.

"Why don't I walk with you inside—you know, be your wingman?" she repeated, holding out her hand as if he was some kind of wayward toddler.

He was unsure if he should be excited or offended by the way she was treating him, but he had to admit the look she was giving him was far more comforting than the one from a few minutes before, when she had found him holding the gun.

He slipped his hand into hers, and she jerked, almost as if she hadn't expected him to take her up on her offer. She let go again at once, but not before his father gave him a look of surprise. Rainier was sure his own expression mirrored his dad's.

This woman continually surprised him. He'd heard so many things about parole officers when he'd been behind bars. From the stories that got filtered down to him, most sounded like real hard asses, but not Laura. Sure, she had a hard edge to her and she was a no-nonsense kind of lady, but there was something equally soft, almost maternal about her. That softness made him wonder if she had a child.

He wasn't sure if he should ask, especially now that she had agreed to take his side and cover up his role in discovering the remains. He didn't want to compromise her emotionally any more than necessary. More than that, from the second they had met she had made it clear to him that there was going to be nothing more than professional civility between them.

She walked ahead of him, leading the way back to the house as the sound of the sirens grew louder. As they approached the door, his mother and his brother Wyatt's fiancée, Gwen, stepped outside.

Rainier glanced down at his mud-covered coat as he tried to wipe the dirt from his hands.

"What's going on?" his mother asked, peering out in the distance toward the approaching police cars.

Laura smiled, but the action was forced and tight. "No worries, I just jumped the gun—" Her mouth gaped open for a moment as she must have realized what she had said.

"We just found something a little odd, and Ms. Blade thought it best if we got a crew out here to investigate it," Rainier interjected.

"Investigate what?" Gwen asked. "And where's your father?"

Rainier turned and looked toward the barn. "He was going to greet the deputies when they arrived. You don't think it's gonna be Wyatt, do you?"

Gwen frowned. "He wouldn't come roaring out here with the sirens on. He's been coming out here enough lately that he would know not to create any kind of scene for the neighbors. It's gotta be somebody else," she said, motioning toward the SUV hurtling their way. As it drew nearer, Rainier could see there was a patrol unit without its lights on following in its wake.

The SUV pulled to a sudden stop, skidding on the ice in the parking lot. A woman, her dark hair pulled into a tight ponytail, jumped out of the car and made her way over to them, with Merle hurrying after her.

"There's Wyatt," Gwen said, ignoring the woman and motioning toward the vehicle just pulling into the lot.

"Who's she?" Rainier whispered.

"New recruit. Her name's Penny Marshall." Gwen frowned, and the look on her face held a trace of jealousy, but he wasn't sure why his soon-to-be sister-in-law would have anything to worry about. Wyatt, above all things, was a good man.

His brother stepped out of the second car. "Penny, wait up. Jeez, woman, you seriously need to slow down. This is my family."

The patrolwoman turned around. "Hey, if you want to drive like some old fart, that's on you. For all you knew, someone's life could have been in danger out here, and you were driving like it wasn't some kind of emergency."

"If someone's life was in danger, Penny, we would have been told about it. That's what dispatch is for. I've told you before, there's no good reason to put our lives at risk when a situation doesn't dictate it."

"Okay, Deputy Fitzgerald," the woman said, but from the tone of her voice Rainier could tell that she was just playing along and fully intended to keep living her way with or without Wyatt's approval.

Rainier liked Penny already. From the looks of her, she was in her early twenties, and from the sound of his brother's exasperated voice, straight out of the academy.

Wyatt's lips puckered and his face darkened as he looked up and noticed him standing there. "So you made it back to the ranch?" He slammed his car door with a little too much force, clearly pissed off. "Is your homecoming the reason for our appearance?"

Rainier swallowed back the growl that percolated up from his core. He had known this was going to be the closest thing to a welcome he was going to get from his brother, but his expectations paled in comparison to the reality.

Or maybe it wasn't the lack of welcome he was upset with, but rather the reality that his brother had been correct in his assessment—he was in fact the reason they had been called. But Rainier would never give Wyatt the satisfaction of once again being right in assuming the worst about him.

"It's good to see you, too, brother," he said, trying to temper his disappointment before it had the chance to pepper his voice.

"Wyatt, Penny," Laura said, giving each an acknowledging wave. "Thank you so much for coming on such short notice. There was no reason for you to rush. In fact, if you have somewhere else to be, you are welcome to come back later."

From the stress in her voice, even Laura had to have known how futile and ridiculous she sounded. If there was somewhere else for the deputies of Mystery to be, they would have been there, but it wasn't a town that was usually fraught with crime.

"Laura, you know if you're calling we're going to come running." Wyatt chuckled as he came closer and gave Gwen a quick peck on the cheek. "Though I have to admit, I did drive a little quicker knowing that my fiancée would be here waiting for me."

Gwen smiled, the jealousy disappearing from her features.

It was nice to see his brother in a relationship, but it was strange to see him act so smitten. Wyatt had always been the serious kind, and watching him loosen up in his presence made Rainier wonder if there was still hope for them to fix their relationship. Then again, Gwen and Wyatt loved each other, and he wasn't sure he could say his brother loved him.

"The dispatcher reported that there was some kind of disturbance, something about a parole violation?" Penny asked, looking directly at Rainier.

"No, no. Everything's all right," Laura said with a bit too much indifference. "Actually, it had nothing to do with parole violation. Your dispatcher must've gotten it all wrong."

"Wyatt," Merle exclaimed as he came walking around the side of the barn. "What took you so long?"

Wyatt laughed. "We were worried you fell down or something. Didn't want you getting hurt," he teased.

Their father answered with a long laugh. "Nah, I just found something behind the barn Laura thought you and your friend would want to check out. It's probably nothing, just some old animal bones. In fact, if you guys want to get going, I'm sure we can sweep this right under the rug."

"Why does everyone want us to leave all of a sudden? We just got here," Penny said. "Is this always the way you guys greet one another?"

Eloise's cheeks reddened. "Oh, dear, Penny, don't start thinking that. We're nothing like that around here. We love our boys. We just understand how busy you all can get, being the pillars of this community and all."

"Laying it on a little thick, Mom, aren't you?" Wyatt asked, raising a brow. "Dad, why don't you go ahead and show me those 'old animal bones.'"

Merle glanced over at him, as if trying to decide exactly what to say or not say to Wyatt about their discovery. Rainier shook his head ever so slightly, reaffirming their decision to keep his role in the findings quiet. It wasn't that he was being selfish, no. It was just clear that his brother had so much resentment toward him that if he caught a single whiff of his involvement, Rainier's hope for a life surrounded by family again would be as good as over.

Chapter Five

Laura wasn't sure she really believed that Rainier was as innocent as he and his father proclaimed him, but if she sent him back to prison, it would be an all-time record for the shortest turnaround. In her department, her friend Jim held the current record of three days before his parolee was sent back, after he'd been found in possession of a large amount of heroin. It was a running joke that the parolee had turned back to drugs after spending a day with Jim.

She could just imagine what the guys around the office would say if they learned that after only a matter of hours she'd found her parolee elbows deep in mud, holding a weapon with human remains at his feet. And that was nothing compared to what her father, the high-powered attorney Dennis Blade Esq., would say if he found out Rainier and the Fitzgerald clan were once again in trouble. He'd made it clear to her that he had nothing good to say about the Fitzgeralds.

She couldn't understand her dad's dislike of them. Though things were tense between Wyatt and Rainier, she could still feel a resounding warmth. And the fact that Merle would go to such lengths to help his son keep out of more trouble spoke volumes about his character.

Laura's father hadn't told her why he held such animosity toward the Fitzgeralds, only that they weren't to be trusted.

Then again, she'd never been very good at following her dad's advice.

Hopefully, this time it wouldn't come back to bite her, but the knot in her gut told her there was a very good chance it could.

Wyatt and Penny disappeared behind the barn, following Merle. Maybe that was what the knot was all about—what they were about to find. No doubt the place would be filled with their investigation and forensics team, and the coroner would soon arrive. Then the questions would start. She'd have to keep her story straight, and she'd never been one for lying.

"Laura, how about you and I go ahead and step inside." Mrs. Fitzgerald motioned for her to follow her into the house. "Unless you need to get running."

The word *running* echoed in the air, almost as though someone had struck a bell. No matter how badly she wanted to leave the ranch and resume her normal life, she couldn't go anywhere. They would have questions for her about her involvement, and if she left, she would only fall under further scrutiny.

"I could go for a cup of coffee," Laura agreed.

"So could I," Rainier said, but not before darting one more glance after his brother.

They made their way back inside. Though it hadn't been that long since Laura had been in the kitchen, with everything that had happened in the last hour, it felt as if days had passed. As she made her way through the living room, the sparkle of silver bows atop colorful presents under the Christmas tree caught her eye. There were piles of wrapped gifts—red, green, blue and even a stack of pink ones adorned with Disney princesses.

"Do you have grandchildren, Mrs. Fitzgerald?" she asked, gazing toward the princesses in her best attempt to mask the elephant in the room—the coming investigation.

Eloise beamed. "Just one for now, a beautiful little girl named Winnie. She, Christina and Waylon should be home in a couple of days. He's in the army, working as an MP, and they've been living at the base. I couldn't be more proud of them."

"I'm sure. That's something to be quite proud of," Laura said, but as she spoke she noticed the way

Rainier's entire body seemed to tense as they mentioned familial pride and accolades.

"They're going to get married soon." Mrs. Fitzgerald reached over and gave Gwen's hand a quick squeeze. "Just like my Gwen and Wyatt, and Whitney and Colter. I was hoping that we could have one big wedding over the holidays—you know, put everything bad behind us and use it to start the New Year off with something to really celebrate. Whitney and Colter have been in Spokane, getting everything they think they're going to need. She sent me a picture of her dress the other day. It's just beautiful."

So all the brothers were engaged, except Rainier. Laura had an idea how he must be feeling. Both her sisters were spoken for, but not her. Her mother had made talking about her failing love life into one of her favorite pastimes. And she loved nothing more than giving Laura regular style hints. Last week's had been that she should dye her hair, as she was starting to, as her mother put it, "get a little less shiny…you know, that happens as we ladies age."

Laura had no idea how dying her hair would make it shinier, but she doubted her mom had meant it as anything other than another jab at her aging-spinster lifestyle. She was the same with her sister—which was part of the reason the three of them rarely had anything to do with one another. Recalling her mother's words nearly made her groan aloud, but she checked herself. Whether her mother knew it or not, Laura had no intention of living a life completely devoid of love from the opposite sex. She just had no desire to have a relationship her family knew anything about. She hadn't forgotten how poorly it had gone the last time she'd brought a man around.

The other ladies made their way into the kitchen, while Rainier walked over to the Christmas tree and ran his fingers reverently over one of the boughs, rolling the needles between his fingertips. His simple action made Laura smile.

He had missed so much in the last couple years. The closest he had probably been to a Christmas tree had been seeing them in pictures in the magazines that had been passed around his unit.

"Did you miss this?" she asked, gesturing around the room at the holiday trappings.

She suddenly realized how alone the two of them were, and it made her feel something almost like attraction toward him. She tried to stuff the feeling away. There could be none of that nonsense.

Maybe she'd identified her feelings incorrectly. Maybe it was just that she pitied him. If that was the case, she couldn't fall into the trap of letting her empathy for him morph into something it shouldn't be.

"You know, growing up, I used to love Christmas," Rainier said. "We always had a tree like this one—spruce. Those and ponderosa pine grow all over in this area. It was such a big deal to go pick one out. We'd spend all day in the woods, Dad pointing out what he thought was the perfect tree and my mother inevitably shooting each and every one of them down. It was like a game between the two of them, and it would only come to an end when the daylight faded and they were forced to compromise."

That was a far cry from her family's out-of-the-box trees that they had thrown together each year in just a matter of minutes. One year they had even plastic-wrapped the tree with the ornaments still on, so they wouldn't have to bother decorating it again the next year.

"We would have hot chocolate and s'mores that my mother would warm up on the heater on the dashboard," Rainier continued, as he picked up a red ornament that had fallen to the floor and rehung it on a branch.

"That sounds really special," Laura said, not quite sure if she should interrupt his reminiscing.

He nodded, but she could tell from the distant look on his face that his mind was in the past.

"It really was." He turned to face her, and she could see a glistening in his eyes that hadn't been there before. "I just can't believe that I'm at risk of losing them all again."

Oh, so that was what this was—some veiled attempt to pull at her heartstrings in order to make sure she wasn't tempted to change her mind about his fate. She wouldn't let him play that game, either.

"You have it all wrong if you think you can make me your mark," she said, taking two steps back from him.

"Huh? What are you talking about?" he asked.

"You can't try and manipulate me to get what you want. I know all about your kind."

"*My* kind?" He spat the words. "You mean convict, or do you mean orphans?"

He was trying to pick a fight. It was a good diversionary tactic from the real issue at hand, but she wasn't going to let him pull that one over on her, either.

"I'm just saying that you're not the first ex-con to think he's smarter than me."

Or hardly the first man who thought himself smarter than me, either, but she bit her tongue before she let the words slip from her. She didn't want to come off like some scorned woman. She wasn't anything of the sort, but Rainier needed to remember his place—and his place, right now, was under her thumb.

"If I was smart, the last place I'd be right now is here." He stared at her.

"If push came to shove, if a deputy found out I'd lied for you, I would likely be charged with accessory after the fact," she whispered, just loudly enough for him, but not the women in the kitchen, to hear. "That would mean we would both be headed to prison. Have you thought about that?"

"I know what you did back there was a gamble," he said, tipping his chin toward the barn outside. "Your sacrifice doesn't go unnoticed. You can trust me when I tell you that I had nothing to do with that body."

He moved toward her, and she carefully stepped back until her legs pressed against Mrs. Fitzgerald's '80s model velveteen sofa. The little hairs of the couch upholstery jabbed into the back of her calves, but it was nowhere near as uncomfortable as Rainier was making her when he looked at her like he was now…a look of compassion, respect and maybe something more.

"You have to know that I would never compromise you like that," he added. "Though I've only known you…what? A couple of hours? I believe you're a good person. You're not the kind of woman who would risk everything if she didn't think a person was telling the truth."

The little zing she had felt for him returned, making her wonder if she would ever be able to control her body's responses whenever Rainier said something that made her want to smile.

He moved so close that the only way she could get away from him was by sitting on the sofa, so she plopped down in a most unladylike fashion—complete with a little *oomph* as the air rushed from her lungs.

"I've been wrong before, Rainier," Laura said, gripping her hands in her lap so as to not reach out and touch him.

Thankfully, he stopped his advance and glanced back at the tree. "We all make mistakes, Laura. No one more than me."

"So you agree that what you did to your father was wrong?"

"It wasn't wrong to do what I did. My biological mother and father may have been the worst parents on the planet. I don't even know how I made it out of there alive." He sighed. "How much do you know about my real parents?"

She had done her research on Rainier Fitzgerald, but it seemed that all his records had started when he'd been about sixteen and had gotten his first speeding ticket. His file had been dotted with a few misdemeanors, just the odd fine here and there that often came with a rambunctious teenager; that was, until the assault on his biological father in some low-end beer joint on the south end of town.

"Not much," she said, shaking her head.

"That night in the bar, when the assault happened, it had been a long time coming." Rainier turned away from her and went back to studying the tree. "My birth father was an evil man. He did things that should have sent him to prison and kept him there until his dying day, but instead, he got off scot-free… And in the end, I was the one sent away. Life has a wicked sense of humor."

She wanted to ask what exactly his father had done, but before she could, there was a knock on the door.

Mrs. Fitzgerald came shuffling out of the kitchen, a white apron tied around her waist and what looked to be fresh flour on her hands. She smiled at them as more knocking reverberated through the room.

"Be right with you," she called, wiping her hands on her apron. "I don't know why they bother knocking. If the police are done, I would hope that Wyatt would know to just come right on in," she said, more to herself than to them.

She opened the door and her hands dropped to her sides and she stumbled backward. "What are you doing here, William?"

There, standing in the doorway, was a sour-faced man in a business suit. As he looked inside, he smiled, and the action was as crisp and polished as the rest of his exterior.

"I thought it was high time that I stopped by the ranch and said hello," William Poe said. He nodded toward Laura. "How goes it, Ms. Blade? Your father mentioned that you were going to be poking your head in at the ranch from time to time, thanks to the family jailbird. You know, if it were up to me there would be more than one Fitzgerald prison bound."

The man looked as out of place at Dunrovin as a fox in a henhouse, and just as predatory.

"What are you really doing here, William?" she asked, getting up from the couch. As she did so she made sure to pull her skirt just a bit lower on her knees. The man had a reputation, and she didn't want him leering at her.

He opened his jacket and withdrew a letter. On the front, in big bold red letters, were the words *Final Notice*.

"Something was incorrectly sent to my house. I think it belongs to you all." He flipped the letter toward Mrs. Fitzgerald, but she didn't bother to try and catch it, and it fell to the floor at her feet.

"Why would you be getting our mail, Mr. Poe?" Eloise asked, her voice taking on a dangerous edge that Laura wouldn't have imagined the woman capable of unless she had heard it for herself.

"Well, Mrs. Fitzgerald, I would hardly know," William said, a sleazy smile spreading over his face. "But from that note on the front, I thought it better make its way into your hands." He nudged the envelope with his shoe, leaving tread marks on the paper. "I'd hate to stand in the way of justice being served. You know me. I've always tried to be helpful."

"We know you to be a thorn in our side," Mrs. Fitzgerald retorted.

Rainier walked over to the man. "Why don't you just get the hell out of here?" he said, pushing him back out the door.

"How dare you touch me," William said, his tone filled with hatred.

"What was that old commercial... *Reach out and touch someone*?" Rainier asked with a wicked laugh. "You're lucky all I did was touch you. The next time you set foot on this ranch, you are going to wish that *all* I did was touch you."

"You are going to wish that you never laid your hands on me." William readjusted his suit jacket in what Laura assumed was his best attempt to save his ego. "I'd threaten to sue, but based on what you're about to learn, we both know that you and your family wouldn't have the money to pay me if I won, anyway." He laughed, the room filling with the foul sound.

William turned toward Laura. "You know, if you were like your father, you would save yourself some time and just arrest Rainier now."

Her stomach clenched. Had he seen something? Had he witnessed her lying for Rainier?

"There's no way that man is going to stay out of trouble. In fact, I bet that's why the police are outside, isn't it? Are they just waiting to arrest him?"

William continued on, seemingly unaware of the questions raging through her. "It wouldn't surprise me. This family is nothing but trash."

"You know what, William? I think Rainier was right," Laura said, as she walked over to the doorway. "You need to get gone and stay gone." She slammed the door in the man's face.

As she did, she knew it would come back to haunt her. But right now she didn't need anyone to tell her who or what the Fitzgeralds were. To her, they were just another family that needed her help.

Chapter Six

The affection Rainier felt for Laura had grown tenfold in a matter of seconds. The last thing he had expected was for her to stand up to William Poe, his family's arch nemesis.

He watched as she leaned over and picked up the envelope from the floor, her skirt pulling tight as she moved, making him want her just that much more.

He forced himself to look away. His family didn't need any more drama right now. Since he'd gotten home today they'd found a body, he'd nearly been sent to prison and now William. Rainier hated to imagine what was coming just around the corner. Though, admittedly, if it somehow turned into having Laura in his bed, he wasn't sure that he would mind so much…as long as no one found out. If his mother ever discovered that they were sleeping together, it would probably be the thing that would push her over the edge.

She walked back to Eloise and handed her the letter.

His mom stood still, staring at the door as if she was just waiting for it to open and William to come strutting back inside. The letter in her hands trembled.

"Mom," he said gently. "Mom, why don't you sit down?" He walked over to her and, taking her by the arm, led her to the couch and helped her settle there.

Her gaze never moved from the door.

"Do you mind if I take a look at the letter?" he asked.

She lifted her hand, motioning for him to take it, but said nothing.

He'd never seen her like this, at least not since the day he'd been sentenced. The memory of her sitting in the wooden stands of the courthouse made shivers run down his spine. He'd vowed he would never make her feel like that again, yet here they were... although this time he wasn't entirely sure it was his fault. William's appearance at his family's home had to simply be a coincidence—at least he hoped so.

On the other hand, William had mentioned that he'd known Rainier was being released. Maybe he had planned his arrival to coincide in hopes that his homecoming could be ruined. Maybe it was Wil-

liam's hope that they'd never be happy again. Little
had he known that their day had already been ruined.

Now it was up to Rainier to fix what he could,
and help them all to move past what they couldn't.

He took the envelope from his mother. It was ad-
dressed to the ranch, care of his parents. When he
tore it open, a letter fell out, with the same red letter-
ing as on the envelope. It read *Final Notice*.

He pulled open the letter and saw it was from
the county. As he read the words on the page, they
seemed to blend together into a jumbled mess of
lines and swirls as he tried to understand how "back
taxes" and "working ranch taxation rates" had re-
sulted in "Payment due on or before December 31.
If not paid in full, a lien will be placed against the
property for $150,489."

The number rolled around on his tongue like a
sour grape. His family couldn't owe that much. There
had to be some kind of mistake. Where would they
get that kind of money?

According to his mother's letters over the last few
months, they had been barely scraping by, and it was
only because of the Yule Night festival that they had
managed to pay their bills for the month. Now this?

He looked to his mom, who was still staring at
the door.

Was it possible that she had known what was in

the letter? Had she known this day was coming, and that was why she had turned in on herself as she had?

He glanced back down at the page. There had to be a way to file for an extension—something, anything they could do to give themselves more time.

The taste in his mouth grew more putrid as he read the last line of the body of the letter:

"…an auction will occur if owners fail to remit all sums due by above date."

"What does it say?" Gwen asked, leaning against the doorjamb that led from the living room from the kitchen.

Rainier wasn't sure how he should handle things, but somehow telling Gwen the truth didn't seem like the best option. In fact, telling anyone what he had just read seemed about as much fun as chewing off his own hand.

"Do you mind taking care of Mother, Gwen?" he asked, motioning toward the couch. "Mom, do you want a cup of tea or something?"

She nodded, finally pulling her gaze away from the door. "Earl Grey, please, Gwen." She gave a half smile as she returned to the land of the living and false strength.

"I'll give her a hand in there," Laura said, taking Gwen by the arm as they made their way into the kitchen. "That way you two can have a moment."

He gave her an acknowledging tip of the head

and sat down beside his mother on the couch. He moved the letter so she could see it. "Did you know about this?"

She took it from his hands and, opening the reading glasses that hung from a cord around her neck, she slid them on and started to read.

Eventually she tried to speak, but the words came out in a smattering of syllables and garbled sounds, until she finally stopped struggling and simply shook her head.

"What about Dad?"

She shook her head again.

"Is this even real? How could you be getting a final notice of something due next week if you didn't even know about this?"

"I'm sure it's real," she said, her voice filled with cold resignation. "If I've learned anything about William Poe, it's that he's capable of whatever he wishes. He has and will do everything in his power to try to tear the family and this place apart. He's not going to stop until he succeeds."

Rainier pointed to the letter. "But something like this had to be in the works for months. Why now? Why is he coming after us with this?"

"He's never been a fan of ours, but I don't know why. For the last few years we managed to keep him at bay, but once he became the county tax appraiser, we knew that our days might be numbered. Then with everything that's happened…it's only gotten worse. I told you about his brother, Daryl, and the fire in my letters, yes?"

He nodded.

William had to have some kind of vendetta—something that must have gone deeper than his wife dying at the hands of his crazed former sister-in-law, but Rainier could only guess what was behind it.

"I have to put a stop to this, to him." He stood up and made his way to the door.

"No, Rainier, you're not going to do or say anything that will stop him. William is like a dog with a bone right now. All we can do is hope…"

"And get a goddamned good lawyer, someone who isn't afraid to take the bastard down," he said.

"I'm sure we'll try. But Rainier…you have to know that this may be the end of Dunrovin. We are all getting so tired of fighting. Maybe this is just the world's way of letting us know that it's time to move on. To get a new dream."

"No, Mom, don't talk like that. You just have some asshat who thinks he can do and say what he wants without repercussions." He opened the door. William was standing beside his Mercedes, talking to Penny.

"Officer Marshall, I hope you are planning on escorting that man from our property," Rainier said, charging toward the two as Wyatt and his father made their way back from behind the barn.

"Actually, Rainier, Mr. Poe was just asking me a few questions about my job." ·

"Nothing about why you are here?"

Penny slid William a look that made it clear that was exactly what he had been pressing her about. And knowing about the kind of man William was, Rainier was sure that he was making a solid effort at making a pass on the twenty-something woman, as well.

"Something going on here?" Wyatt asked, coming closer and sensing the tension in the air.

"I was just making sure that William here got in his car and left. He ain't welcome," Rainier said, pointing toward Poe like he was something a horse had left behind.

"If you think I want to spend my free time in this hellhole, you have me all wrong. I have much better things to do. There's money to be made. I told you, I was here as a personal favor. That will be the last time I try to do something nice for you people," William said, adding an edge of pitifulness to his voice in what Rainier assumed was his attempt to play the victim.

"You and I both know what was in that letter, and you took great pride and enjoyment in bringing it here. You did it for yourself. You wanted to witness the results of that bomb firsthand."

William laughed, the sound echoing through the evening. "You must think that I'm the epitome of evil. I can assure you, Rainier, that I'm not the villain you and your family seem to have made me out to be." He reached down and took Penny's hand and gave it a quick peck. "I'm sorry you had to witness all of this, Officer Marshall. On the other hand, it is good that you know exactly the kind of hatred that this family seems all too capable of."

Penny pulled back her hand, but not before Rainier noticed a little flush in her face.

He really couldn't understand what women saw in this guy. He was clearly nothing but a selfish, lowlife con artist.

William walked away, giving Penny one more tip of the head before he got into his car and drove off. As the light from his taillights disappeared in the distance, Wyatt turned toward Rainier. "What was all that about?"

He looked to Penny, hoping his brother would take the silent cue that they shouldn't be talking about William in front of what could possibly be one of his many love-struck followers.

Wyatt gave him a small, almost imperceptible nod.

"What did you guys find back there?" Rainier

asked, thankful for his brother's understanding. "Are they human remains or animal?"

"Definitely human. And the gun has been in that ground for a while. We got the area cordoned off and tomorrow we'll get our team out here to start excavating the crime scene."

"Crime scene?" Rainier asked, a cold chill running through him.

"Any time there is an unwitnessed death—no matter how long it's been since it happened—we have to treat it like a crime scene."

"Do you have any idea how long the bone has been there? Or who they could have belonged to?"

Wyatt shook his head. "Like I said, we'll have to go over the entire scene with a fine-tooth comb and send in our findings to the medical examiner. But until then there is nothing I can say as to what the findings will be." Wyatt stared at him for a moment. "Is there some reason you are so inquisitive?"

So there it was; his brother's true feelings toward him were rearing their ugly head once again.

"I just want the best for everyone and everything involved here, Wyatt. Can't we call some kind of truce or something?" Rainier waved in the direction William's car had gone. "He's our real enemy…not members of our own family."

"I'm not your enemy, brother, but I do care what happens to this family—and I care when someone, even someone in our ranks, does things that are outside our best interest." Wyatt turned to Penny. "I want you to stay here, retain the chain of custody on this crime scene until Lyle and Steve can come in and conduct their investigation. Don't let anyone, especially him—" he pointed at Rainier "—close to the scene."

His brother stormed off to his patrol car, slamming the door as he got in.

Rainier had no idea how he was going to fix things with his brother, only that he had to, not only for his own sake, but for the sake of his parents. They didn't need to deal with his brother's petty drama, not now.

"If you'll excuse me," said Penny, "I'm just going to get going..." She gave him a look that was half apologetic and yet still held an air of skepticism as to the kind of man he was.

"Yeah, no problem. And don't worry, no matter what my brother thinks, I have no intention of messing around with your crime scene or anything else. In fact, if you need anything—food, whatever—let me know and I can get something to you."

Penny smiled and some of the reservation she seemed to hold for him slipped away. "I appreciate that, Rainier. I'll let you know."

He nodded, and he and his father watched as she walked off. As soon as she was out of earshot, Merle turned toward him. "Now, what was that with William? What was in the letter?"

Rainier cringed. The last thing he wanted to do was break the news to his father about the back taxes. "I think you should talk to Mom. She's pretty upset."

They made their way into the house. Rainier was happy to get in from the cold. He hadn't noticed how it had crept up on him, stealing his heat until his fingers and toes had gone almost completely numb. He squeezed his fists, forcing blood back into his extremities as they made their way into the dining room. Everyone was sitting around the table, and it reminded him of their traditional family suppers, except in this case, no one was smiling.

This was all a far cry from what he had expected to come home to. He couldn't help wondering, as he looked around at the tired and haggard expressions, if maybe everyone would have been better off if he had simply stayed behind bars.

Laura stood up and made her way over to him, just out of earshot from the rest of the family. "Is everything okay outside? Is William gone?"

"You know it."

"Where's Wyatt and his team?"

"His team isn't going to come in until tomorrow. I think they feel a body this old doesn't need a team to come out this late in the night. I think they are planning on hitting it at first light."

"So they don't need to interview us?" A look of relief washed over her.

He shook his head. "No, and don't worry. Everything is going to be fine."

"Even with the letter? Are your parents going to be able to afford this?" she whispered, looking around to make sure no one else could hear her.

He looked to his mother. "I don't think so. Their best hope is to find a good lawyer. They're going to have to fight...and fight hard. But there isn't much time. According to the letter, they have to pay by the end of the year. And by now—you know how the government works—everything is shut down for the year. They're going to have a hell of a time getting in touch with the right people...people who can put a stop to this, or can help them figure out how they should go about fixing it."

Laura nibbled at her lip. "Do they have a lawyer on retainer?"

He shrugged. "I don't think so, but with everything that's happened here, it would be a good idea if they did. Hell, I bet by now they would have some kind of punch card started."

She gave a little laugh, but bit it back. "If they need someone, you know my father...he's a lawyer."

"And apparently a friend of William Poe's?" He gave her a questioning look.

"They work together. You know how it is in small

towns—everyone in the county runs into each other, and it's best that they remain civil. We all just end up using each other." She shifted her weight as if she were trying to rid herself of the burden of what she had just accused the government officials of. "My father is a tough man to get along with, and he may not take on the case, but if you want I can talk to him about all of this."

From the fatalistic but determined look on her face, Rainier could see that this was an offer she never made, and it helped him appreciate her favor that much more.

"If you wouldn't mind…maybe you and I can go tomorrow and I can talk to him, as well. Make him understand all that is happening."

"I'm sorry, Rainier." She looked down at her hands. "But I'm not sure that's the best idea. My father knows about you…what happened. He's not one of your biggest fans. And if we are going to have him as an ally, maybe it's better if someone else comes."

Merle cleared his throat, as though reminding them that they weren't alone. "Laura, if you'd like, Mother and I would love to go and talk to your father."

Laura blushed. "I'm sorry, I didn't mean for you to hear—"

Merle waved her off. "No worries. I…I mean, we appreciate all the help we can get."

"I'll meet you at his office in the morning." She reached over and touched Rainier's upper arm. Having her hand on him felt as good as it felt wrong, but neither of them pulled away. "Why don't you come with us, after all? Even if you're not in the meeting, I'd like to have you there to support your parents… and me."

He smiled. For the first time all day, something was going right.

Chapter Seven

She'd had an inbox full of emails when she'd gotten up this morning; most were about parolees and questions from potential employers. Laura made quick work of them and made a few phone calls, but all she could think about was seeing her father, the ever terrifying Dennis Blade, Esq.

There were many who thought her father charming, service-oriented and willing to go the extra mile. But she had known the other side of him much better—his need to control, to manipulate and use people, and to do whatever it took to get what he wanted. If someone were to ask her if he was a good person, she wasn't sure she could say yes; rather, she would have told them that he was simply a man. He was both good and bad, giving and taking, and though he had faults, he'd always loved her.

Even if that love meant him being a constant source of anxiety in her life.

That anxiety had always been associated with family, which was why the Fitzgeralds were like an enigma—with Rainier's parents' open arms and open minds, the self-sacrifice and generosity of spirit. The only tension came from Rainier and Wyatt, but even she could see that beneath the hurt feelings and animosity was a deep well of love.

It wasn't a long drive to her father's office building in the city, and when she arrived, Rainier, Merle and Eloise were already there. They were standing beside their car, huddled in a little group while they waited for her. She glanced down at her watch and saw she was fifteen minutes early.

She parked beside them, and as her eyes met Rainier's she couldn't help the little jolt of excitement she felt at seeing him again.

"Hey," he said, holding out his hand to help her step from her car.

Though it was in the single digits outside, his hand was warm, making her wonder if his body was reacting to her being near, just as hers was to his presence.

"Hi," she replied, but even to her ears she sounded like an enamored teen, and she chastised herself. She cleared her throat as she tried to collect her emotions, and reminded herself there was nothing between them. "Mrs. and Mr. Fitzgerald," she said, giving his parents a quick wave as she pulled her other hand from Rainier's warm grip.

"Please call us Merle and Eloise," his mother said. "I think we've moved past formalities."

"Absolutely, Eloise." Laura smiled and gave the woman a slight, appreciative nod. "Been here long?"

Rainier shook his head. "Only about ten minutes. We wanted to make sure we had enough time to talk before we went inside."

So he had been outside long enough for his fingers to grow cold. The thought made her grin. Maybe his attraction to her wasn't just something she was imagining. But it was still silly to get her hopes up—or to have any hopes at all, for that matter.

"Did you have something on your mind?" Laura asked, trying to stop herself from thinking about anything that wasn't directly involved with their mission.

Merle and Eloise looked at each other as if they could speak in some silent code after so many years of marriage.

"We just wanted to say we know you're going out of your way to help us," Eloise said. "We appreciate everything you're trying to do, with Rainier included. Yet we understand what a long shot it's going to be, getting us out of trouble with the county."

"I'm sure everything will be all—"

"No, that's it," Eloise interrupted. "It may not turn out how we all hope. We don't want you to be disappointed and feel like you failed if this doesn't work out."

Laura wanted to hug her for being so understanding even in these hard times. It took a higher class of lady to think about others and put their feelings first, when so much was going on in her own world.

Laura wanted to comfort her and tell her that she was wrong, that they would make everything come together and all their troubles disappear, but she couldn't bring herself to lie. Eloise was right, the chances were low, but that didn't mean they had to lose hope. If anything, it was in times like these, when everything seemed so bleak, that having faith and hope was most critical.

"Let's talk to my father first and see what he has to say. He tends to know the right people, at least the kind of people who can make something like this disappear." She wasn't sure if she should tell them about his penchant for being mercurial, especially when it came to his daughter and her requests for help.

Eloise sighed, the sound speaking volumes of relief that Laura's words must have given her. They made their way inside, through the elaborate curly maple doors that led to her father's office lobby. With each step, her nervousness grew, forcing her to wipe her sweaty palm against her skirt. She glanced down at the little wet mark left behind. No doubt her father would notice; he was nothing if not detail oriented.

"Why don't you guys wait right here?" She pointed to the leather sofa and chair set in the reception area, and the family sat down. "I'll be right back."

She walked over to the secretary's desk and was greeted with a smile from the woman sitting there. "Hello, Ms. Blade, your father is expecting you. Would you like me to let him know that you and your friends are here?"

"Please."

She waited as the woman made a call to her father's inner sanctum, and they spoke in hushed tones. From the look on the secretary's face, her father must have been giving her what-for, making Laura's anxiety grow.

"I'll head on in," she said, not waiting for the woman to get off the phone. "I'll come get my friends in a moment. I just need to speak to my father alone."

The woman held out her hand for her to stop, but Laura didn't heed her warning and she strode down the hall and tapped on her father's door. She could hear the phone slamming down on the receiver through the heavy wooden panel.

"Come in, Laura," he said, his baritone echoing through the empty hallway.

She swallowed back her fear and shook out her hands, then made her way inside, careful to close the door behind her.

"Father," she said with a nod. "Thank you for finding time in your schedule to talk to us today."

"Where are your *friends*?" he hissed. "I would think if they were coming here to request representation they would have the decency to at least show up."

"Oh, the Fitzgeralds are here," she said, gesturing toward the lobby. "They're just outside. Before bringing them in, I wanted to speak to you for a moment."

"What about? Them or some other harebrained scheme of yours?"

She wanted to stand up to her dad, to tell him he had no right to be so demeaning toward her, but right now, when she'd come here for a favor, it didn't seem like the right time to start a fight.

"I was hoping we could talk about them and what I would like to see happen with this taxes mess."

"I got the general idea, thanks to your late-night phone call. Don't you remember that I have to get up every morning at 5:00 a.m.?"

So that was the reason he was in such a foul mood today.

"I'm sorry to have disturbed you. That wasn't my intention. I just knew that this all had to be handled as quickly as possible. Though I would think you get phone calls at night quite regularly."

He gave her a heated look that told her she had made another mistake. "I have a call service for a reason. And you know, Laura, there are at least a hundred other things I could be doing with my morning besides dealing with more of your nonsense."

Hopefully he wouldn't go so far as to actually talk about Tanner, they had been down that road a thousand times and she didn't want to rehash what had happened with her ex.

She gritted her teeth. She couldn't be insolent.

"I appreciate you taking the time…as I said. I understand you're busy, but as you know, this is about William Poe. You have to stop him."

Her father chuckled. "William couldn't have done something like this. He doesn't have the power."

"But he knows the right people to make this happen. And explain to me how he could've gotten their mail. It just doesn't seem legal."

He tented his fingers in front of him on his desk and turned slightly in his chair. "That is odd, and as much as I respect William, it is suspicious that he would involve himself in something like this. Either he got sloppy and is playing more of a role than I'd assumed, or he really is innocent."

"I think we both know the answer to the question if William is innocent or guilty."

"You're naive if you think that we're not all a little bit of both. To be successful in life and at business means being able to make choices others aren't capable of, and William certainly is good at his job.

But that doesn't necessarily mean that he is guilty of any wrongdoing."

"But you'll take the case?"

"What you're asking is far more complicated than you can possibly know." Her father put his hands down on his desk. "And we both know that you have a tendency to get wrapped up in things like this—things that you have no business including yourself in. It's just like that mess with Tanner."

Of course he would go there. Whenever she asked for something, and he wanted to say no, he would always go to the subject of her former boyfriend, Tanner.

"He has nothing to do with this, Father."

"He may not, but it's a perfect example of your weaknesses. You always waste your time on losers."

"The Fitzgeralds aren't losers."

Her father snorted. "If they're going against William Poe, then that's exactly what they're setting themselves up to become."

If this was what it was going to be like to work with her father, maybe they would be better off getting another lawyer. But if she went out and faced the Fitzgeralds now, it would deal them a hard blow. They'd rested all their hopes with her and her ability to have a civil conversation with her father, a conversation that could make or break their future.

"Besides, right now public opinion is starting to

turn against the family, and that makes it even harder to take this all the way. Especially with this new finding on the ranch—that set of remains is going to be the straw that breaks the camel's back when it comes to the public being on their side."

"How do you know about the remains?" she asked, shock riddling her voice. Wyatt and his team were out at the ranch now, and they likely hadn't even finished up yet—and her father seemed to know all about it.

"Something like that isn't going to stay a secret for long. You and I both know how living in western Montana is. All gossip is just a phone call away. And it's my job to keep a close tab on what you are choosing to do with your life. You can't really think that I'd let you work with convicted felons all day long and not check up on you."

"So you're spying on me?"

Her dad shook his head as if he was growing tired of her. "Laura, I'm your father. No matter what you think of me or my choices, I'm always going to do what I feel is best for you. Even if you don't like it."

She couldn't stand him sometimes. "Dad, I'm old enough to take care of myself. I don't need you constantly looking over my shoulder. I'm an adult."

"If that's true, then take your friends and figure this out yourself." He pointed toward the door. "Mark my words, the Fitzgeralds are in a situation

from which there is no coming back. If they are im-
plicated with this body—if they had anything to do
with this person's untimely death—and you are associated with them, everything you're fighting for
is going to come to an end. You will find yourself in
trouble right next to them. You need to go."

"They had nothing to do with this person's death,"
she said, ignoring his order for her to leave. "For all
we know, the person has been dead for years. Long
before the family owned the ranch."

"From what I heard, that may not be the case. Regardless, you need to stay away."

Her father had this all wrong. No matter what
he had heard or what he assumed, the Fitzgeralds
weren't the antagonists here. No, this family hadn't
done anything wrong. Eloise and Merle had gone
above and beyond in their attempts to take in foster
kids, adopt Rainier and his brothers and run a guest
ranch that brought smiles to their guests' faces. They
weren't murderers. They weren't tax evaders. They
were always trying to do the right thing, and she had
no idea why her father couldn't see them for who
they really were.

"If I show you, if I can prove that the Fitzgeralds
had nothing to do with do with this fiasco with these
human remains, would you agree to help them?"

He sat quietly for a moment. "We'll see what

you're capable of. But let me say it again—you need to get off the boat before it sinks."

That was as close to help as she was going to get with her father for now, and the only thing sinking was her stomach. She turned and started to make her way out of his office.

"And Laura, be wary of William Poe. He's got his fingers in a lot of pots."

She gave a cynical laugh as she thought about William's reputation for seducing women. She was sure that was not what her father was referencing, but she couldn't get the image out of her mind.

Her laugh echoed down the hall, and as Laura made her way to the waiting room, Eloise stood up at the sound and looked toward her.

"So everything went well in there?" She smiled. "Is he ready for us to come and talk to him?"

Laura wanted to tell Eloise the truth, that they were barely hanging on by a thread to the hope that he would involve himself in their case, but she couldn't bring herself to do it.

"Actually, he's up-to-date on the situation. I'm hoping he's going to start looking into things."

She felt okay as she skirted around the truth. What she had said wasn't a bold-faced lie, rather a twist on words. For now, that would have to work.

"In the meantime, we need to make sure that Dunrovin focuses on clearing its name and restoring its place as a premier guest ranch."

"We can do that. Isn't that right, Merle?" Eloise said, joy speckling her voice and making Laura feel even worse about keeping the truth from them.

As they turned to leave, Rainier walked with her. As soon as they were out the doors, he took her hand and slowed her to a stop, while his parents walked ahead of them to the car.

"He isn't going to help us, is he?"

The blood drained from her face. There was no way he could have heard her and her father talking, so how could Rainier possibly know what had happened behind those closed doors? "I... He...he doesn't think there's a way to win the case—no matter if he or another lawyer takes this on," she said, letting the words pour from her. "And he's worried that the body is going to make the law come down on your family even harder, regardless of your brother's role in the department. The only way we even have a fighting chance of sorting this all out and getting any lawyer to take this case on is if we can prove that you all had nothing to do with those remains."

Rainier sucked in a long breath, as though composing himself before speaking. "Okay." He nodded. "You said I needed a job as a condition of my parole.

From this moment on, my job is going to be to help Wyatt get to the bottom of this. Come hell or high water, my family is going to get the help they need."

Chapter Eight

When they made it back to the ranch, Wyatt and his team of investigators—which consisted of Lyle and Steve, who looked oddly like Andy Griffith and Barney Fife—were screening dirt that they had dug up from around the spigot. From the looks of things, they hadn't found anything else, which made a profound sense of relief wash through Rainier. If they couldn't find any more bones, that meant there wouldn't be a whole lot for the medical examiner to study, which hopefully meant the case would go cold and soon be forgotten.

If only they could get that lucky.

He looked over at Laura as she got out of her car, thankful that she had agreed to come back to the ranch after she'd made a few phone calls to make herself available. He couldn't believe how helpful she was being, or how many risks she was taking in helping him and his family. He doubted that she was normally this involved with her parolees, but maybe he was wrong. Maybe this was just her way—giving, selfless and filled with the spirit of altruism.

He couldn't deny that he'd gotten lucky in being assigned a parole officer like her. She wasn't anything like what he'd expected—some middle-aged, balding guy with a chip on his shoulder and a heavy drinking problem. Rainier chuckled at the thought of how far from the stereotype she was.

She closed the door to her car and turned to him. "Did you talk to your brother yet?"

He shook his head. The entire drive home from the city he had been trying to come up with a way, or something to say, that could mend the fences with his brother. Yet he had nothing, and the closer they got to the ranch, the more his nervousness had amplified. "Everything is going to be okay, Rainier," Laura said as she walked over to him. "Your parents told him what was going on, right?"

He looked toward the ranch house, where his parents had disappeared when they had gotten home. They had talked at length on the ride back, including about how thankful they were to have Laura's help, but the one thing no one had spoken of was what they had said to Wyatt.

Rainier cringed as he thought about the possibility that they hadn't mentioned the back taxes to Wyatt, and what would happen if he had to be the one to break the news. It would only give his brother more of an excuse to despise him.

"I dunno," he said.

"Let's just talk to Wyatt and see how it plays out," Laura said. From the way she wrung her hands in front of her, Rainier wondered if she was even more nervous than him.

He watched her as she walked toward the barn and the crew. Lyle was standing over the screens, pushing a clod of dirt through the mesh. He looked up as they approached and wiped his gloved hand over his brow, leaving behind a line of dirt complete with bits of rotting grass.

"Hey, Lyle. How's it going?" Rainier asked, trying to make ground with his brother's team.

"Slow and steady," he said, sounding every bit as stoic and relaxed as he looked.

"With something like this, I'm sure that you are going about it right." Rainier gave an approving nod. "You guys find anything interesting yet?"

Lyle glanced toward Steve, who was standing in the water-filled hole. A thin layer of ice had collected around the edges during the night and Steve lifted his hands and blew into them in an attempt to stave off the cold. He was wearing a pair of neoprene chest waders and a coat, but from the blue hue of his lips, the only thing the man probably wanted to do was get out of the freezing water.

"Steve, you know where Wyatt is?" Lyle asked.

The half-frozen man shook his head. "He disappeared a little while ago. Not sure where he went."

Rainier tried to tell himself that it wasn't strange that his brother would leave these two men alone and not tell them where he had gone. He could have been doing any number of things, or maybe he was talking to their parents or something, but there was a part of Rainier that went on high alert. Wyatt was always the kind of guy to see things through to the end.

"If you see him, would you let him know that we're looking for him?" Laura asked.

Lyle answered with a nod and went back to pushing another piece of dirt through the mesh.

They walked back around the barn. "That was odd, wasn't it?" she asked in a whisper.

"Either they found something and they didn't want to tell us, or Wyatt had warned them not to speak to us about anything," Rainier said.

"To be honest, I'm a little surprised that your brother is even heading this investigation. I would think it would be some kind of conflict of interest for him to be involved. You know, this being the family's ranch and all," Laura said.

"Well, you know how it is. His department isn't all that big. If people walked away from investigations just because they knew someone vaguely involved, every case in the entire town would have to be outsourced." Rainier chuckled. "And maybe that's why he brought Penny along. That way there's another set of hands in case he is ever scrutinized for his role in the investigation."

"You know, if you guys are gonna talk, you should talk a little quieter," Wyatt said, walking out of the barn and wiping his hands on a dirty rag. "The reason I'm heading this investigation is that, unlike you, people trust me. Just because I have some tie to this place doesn't mean that I won't do what is right, or prosecute those that need to be prosecuted—even if it's my own brother."

Rainier tried to control the anger that started to roil within him at the veiled accusation. "Look, I don't have anything to do with this body. I don't know why you think you need to keep threatening me. I'm sorry for what happened with my father. I know that it screwed everything up—probably for you more than anyone else in the family."

"You got that right. Do you know the kind of crap I have to take from the guys at the station? The questions I've had to field about having a felon as a brother?"

"Wyatt, I've done my time. I've paid for my crime. Why do you think I need to keep paying?"

"It's not about wanting to make you keep paying. We both know it's not that simple. I know what kind of person you are, Rainier. We both know that you have a hair-trigger and it's going to get you back in trouble in no time."

"Can't you see that I've changed?" he countered. "If I was still the man I used to be, do you think I'd be standing here and just taking it as you talk to me like you are?"

Laura reached up and put her hand on Rainier's arm, calming him. "Wyatt, I understand that you and your brother have had a lot happen between you two, but don't you think that you should start fresh?"

Wyatt peered at her, a look of confusion and disbelief on his face. "Are you serious? You should know better than anyone what the return rates are for prisoners. People don't change. They are who they are."

Laura hand slipped down Rainier's arm, releasing him and making him wonder if Wyatt's words were making her question her approach. The anger within him grew, threatening to spill out. He wanted to tell his brother to go to hell, that it didn't matter what he thought, and to chastise him for screwing up the only thing he had going for him—Laura's belief that maybe he was worth helping. It had been a long time since he'd had an advocate besides his parents; and yet Wyatt thought it best that he stand in his way.

On the other hand, maybe his brother was right. Rainier could check his anger now, but how long would he be able to? And what if he saw his birth father again or he was put in a situation like before? He couldn't honestly tell himself, or anyone else for that matter, that he would make a different decision than the one he had. Maybe he really hadn't changed, after all.

"Wyatt," Laura said, "you're right. I have learned a lot on my job. I have learned that some people are incapable of change, but I know that your brother is different. He has a chance. But he won't if he has to fight against the people who are supposed to love him the most. When people don't have a soft place to land after prison, if they aren't given the tools to succeed, that's when they find trouble. You want your brother to succeed, don't you?"

The tight, ferocious lines around Wyatt's lips softened and he seemed to relax. He sighed as he glanced at Rainier. "Look, I don't want to stand in your way. You know I don't. You know I love you. And you have to know that I understand that we all make mistakes. Given, mine haven't been the same caliber of yours, but—"

"You're putting him down again," Laura said. "You're not helping."

"You're right," Wyatt said. "Rainier, I'm sorry. That wasn't intentional. It's just… It's going to take me some time to get over this."

Rainier couldn't believe the words that came out of his brother's mouth. No matter what he would have said to Wyatt, it wouldn't have been nearly as effective as Laura's cool, calm and logical approach. He was impressed with her, and it made him wonder how her parolees tended to fare compared to those of other parole officers.

"Thanks, man. I totally get it. And know that I truly am sorry for making you go through crap. I didn't realize… I *hadn't* realized how much it had affected you."

"If you want me to get past this, you need to promise me that you will do everything in your power not to get into trouble again," Wyatt said.

Rainier's thoughts moved to the investigation and the lie that he and Laura had told. He could only imagine what his brother would say if he learned the truth. "I promise, from this moment on, I'll do my best."

Laura smiled, and it made him wonder if she had thought about their lie, as well, or if she was smiling simply because she had heard his careful maneuvering around it. Or if she wasn't thinking like he was at all, and was simply happy that the brothers were once again back on square footing. Whatever was making her smile, he was glad to see her do it. She was so beautiful when she smiled. Even her blue eyes seemed to sparkle a little bit more when she was happy. He stared at her, unable to look away. It wasn't that she was just breathtakingly beautiful on the outside, with all of her wonderful and luxurious curves, but her soul was equally as intoxicating. She truly was the most enchanting person he'd ever laid eyes on.

And yet she was completely untouchable.

Wyatt threw the dirty rag over his shoulder and ran his hands down his face as he let out an exasperated breath. "By the way, Gwen told me about the letter."

"Good," Rainier said, relieved. "I mean not *good*, but I'm glad she told you," he said, trying to make up for his mistake.

"How did the meeting with your father go?" Wyatt asked.

Laura gave Rainier a look that made it clear she wasn't exactly sure what to tell him.

"I think it's best he knows the truth, even if our parents don't. He's the only other one who can really help us," Rainier said, urging her on.

"Wait. What are you guys talking about? What happened?" Wyatt pressed.

"Let's step into the barn," Rainier said, suddenly all too aware that Lyle and Steve may have been listening.

They followed Wyatt into the barn, and Rainier walked over to the first stall, where his favorite horse, Clark, stood with his head sticking out in greeting. He ran his hands down the horse's cheeks and scratched under his chin. "How's it going, old boy?" he asked as the horse sniffed at him, taking in his scent.

"So what did the lawyer say?" Wyatt pressed.

Rainier turned back. "He feels the same way about me that you do, or *did*. He thinks that Laura is making a mistake getting wrapped up with me and this place. And, well, he doesn't think that he can help us go up against William Poe with everything that's stacked against us."

Wyatt leaned against the table at the front of the barn. "So, we can get another lawyer."

"When it comes to tax law," Laura said, "there's no one better in the state than my father. His firm is fantastic. They can make anything go away. You want him. And besides, according to him, no one else is going to touch anything that goes against Poe. You know what kind of pull he has in the county. No one wants to go toe-to-toe with him."

"That man needs to disappear…" Wyatt said, half under his breath.

Rainier laughed. "Don't say that too loud. People around here are already questioning us. If Poe died… you know every law enforcement agency, including yours, would be down here and taking us all into custody. And even if he did *disappear*, that wouldn't mean that our tax problem would."

"I suppose you're right. We need to fix one major

catastrophe at a time," Wyatt said, crossing his arms over his chest.

"Let's start with this body. Do you think we can just sweep it under the rug?" Rainier asked.

"Not after today..." Wyatt paused. "This morning we found the person's skull. From what I know about forensics, it looked like a man...a man with a gunshot wound to the head."

The breath seeped out from Rainier. No. This couldn't be happening. Not now. Not when they needed to put this behind them.

"If he had a gun with him," Laura said, "couldn't it be possible that the guy committed suicide?"

"Or the killer threw the gun into the hole when he buried the body," Wyatt said. "I mean, a person couldn't bury himself. There had to be someone else involved."

His brother was right. Rainier couldn't believe he had missed such an obvious thing.

"Did you find anything else? Anything that could date it?" he pressed, though he knew he was grasping at straws.

"You want to take a look? I was just bagging it up to send it to the lab," Wyatt said, motioning toward the bag that was sitting on the workbench.

"Sure," Laura said, surprising Rainier with her willingness to see something that could potentially be gruesome.

Wyatt grabbed the bag and, opening it, carefully withdrew the skull. Parts of it were covered in a thin layer of mud, which made it look like something from a movie and less macabre than Rainier had anticipated.

"So if you look right here..." Wyatt turned the skull and pointed to a small hole near where the right ear would have been. "See this?"

Rainier nodded. It was about the size of a dime and the bone around it had been stained an ashy black.

"I'm no expert in forensics, but from what I know about gunshot wounds, I would say that when the gun was fired it had to have been close. I mean, look at these margins," he said, indicating the edge of the wound. "Look at this internal beveling." He turned the skull so they could peer inside the cranium. He pulled out a flashlight and, turning it on, shone it into the empty space where the man's brain had once been. "And if you look here, see this collection of fracturing? That's from the increased pressure that occurs when the bullet moves through the skull."

"What does that all mean? As far as the shooting goes?" Rainier asked, staring at the hairline fractures.

"It's all proof that whoever did this was standing close. Very close."

"So someone executed the guy?" Laura asked, motioning toward the skull.

Wyatt shrugged. "It's hard to say. But what I do know is that if this story gets out to John Q. Public, your father is going to be proved right. People are going to be in an uproar. We've already had enough death at the ranch lately. This is going to push people over the edge. It's going to be hard to prove that we've just been going through a string of bad luck and nothing more sinister is going on."

"Let's not get ahead of ourselves," Rainier said, mostly in an attempt to stop himself from going off the rails. "We still have to wait on the report from the medical examiner, right?"

"Sure," Wyatt said. "And who knows, she'll probably see something I missed. Maybe she can help us make sense of this guy's death. At the very least, she can probably give us a time line."

"How long do you think it's going to take to hear back from her?"

Wyatt shook his head, turning off the flashlight and putting it back into his belt. "It's hard to say. She has the femur and the gun, but until we give her this…" Wyatt shrugged as he set the skull back in the bag. "To be honest, we're hoping to recover more before we go to her. If we do, we'd have more evidence to go on—maybe even find something to point in the direction of anyone else who was involved."

Now all Rainier could hope for was that if someone else was involved in what could have possibly been this man's murder, it wasn't anyone in his family. If it was, they would never clear the Fitzgerald name and there would be no going back.

Chapter Nine

Laura and Rainier walked out of the barn and toward the parking lot. She felt as though she was in a daze after Wyatt's findings. This place and all the people in it seemed to be cursed—and not just over the last month, as she had assumed. From the looks of the human remains, the curse had been looming over the place for years.

It seemed as if no matter what they did, they were never going to break free from the bad luck and torture that the world wanted to put this family through.

She thought of the old saying "You won't be given more than you can handle," and wondered if it was really true. Was this all just a way for Rainier's family to be tested? Was it some ethereal plan put in place to make the family come together? Or maybe it was nothing more than a string of bad luck. No. There had to be a reason behind the madness. This all couldn't be due to some cosmic randomness, but had to be happening for something greater—something that would bring the family joy and happiness in the end.

Or maybe, as her father was always happy to point out, she was being naive.

A white truck with a Dunrovin brand on the driver's-side door pulled into the parking lot. A man and woman she recognized as Rainier's brother Colter, and his fiancée, Whitney, from the ranch's Yule Night festival were inside the extended cab, and as she looked at them they each gave her a warm smile and an excited wave. Rainier stopped and stared.

"You okay?" she asked, seeing the way his eyes seemed to darken thanks to his brother's arrival.

Rainier nodded. "I'm just hoping he's a little bit more welcoming than Wyatt. I don't know if I have any more apologies in me."

She reached over and took his hand. "No matter what happens, I'm here for you. And from their smiles, I'm thinking they're more than happy to see you." As the words slipped from her, she second-guessed them. If Colter had been happy Rainier was home, he wouldn't have been MIA for the last day and a half.

From the scowl on Rainier's face, he must have been thinking along the same lines.

"Let's go say hello," she said, hoping against all hope that this would go better than he was assuming.

He said something unintelligible under his breath, but she pretended not to hear him grumbling and instead led him toward the truck.

Whitney was getting out as they approached.

"Hey, Whit!" she exclaimed.

Whitney's smile widened. "Heya, I'm so glad you're here. I could use an extra set of hands." She glanced down at Rainier's and Laura's entwined hands with the raise of a brow.

Rainier slipped his fingers from hers. Laura tried to ignore the awkwardness that suddenly seemed to fill the air.

"Hey, man. Long time no see," Colter said. He walked over and gave him a quick hug, complete with a slap on the back, almost as though Rainier had simply been on a long vacation. "Whitney, do you know Rainier?" he asked, letting go of his brother and turning toward her.

She stuck out her hand. "I've heard lots of good things."

Rainier looked at his brother as a surprised laugh escaped him. "Really?"

Colter slapped him on the shoulder. "I always got your back, brother," he said with a heartwarming smile.

Standing there and looking at Colter's and Whitney's mirrored expressions of joy, Laura could see why the two were getting married. As Colter moved,

Whitney shifted closer to him, almost as if they were connected by invisible strings that drew them toward each other. She wanted that same kind of love. The kind that was far more than lust, and ran deeper and made silent promises that would last a lifetime.

A new sense of longing filled her as she looked at Rainier. Perhaps he could be the man she needed. Maybe they could have a relationship just like Colter and Whitney's—if they were lucky.

"I'm sorry we weren't here to welcome you home," Colter continued. "We had to run to Spokane to do some wedding shopping. Did you know that there are hundreds of different shades of blue?" He gave Whitney a teasing smile. "And our color is Bondi blue, to be exact."

"Bondi blue?" Laura asked. "What is that?"

"Exactly. You make my point for me," Colter said with a laugh, just as Whitney gave him a playful jab.

"No. Don't get them mixed up in this," she protested. "Technically, Bondi blue is kind of a blue-green color."

"Oh, that sounds beautiful. Is it your only wedding color?" Laura asked.

"That and a gray called—"

"Metropolis," Colter said, finishing Whitney's sentence. "And did you know that they are not always called the same name? It changes with the brand and the designer. So depending on the store, our gray was also called Ash." He turned to Rainier. "Holy crap, I think I just felt my man card rip itself from my wallet."

Rainier laughed as Colter waved for them to step around the side of the truck. He opened the back door and pulled out a stack of garment bags. "Here, take this," he said, handing Rainier four of them. "We'll take 'em to Whitney's office." He motioned toward the main office with his chin.

Laura stepped up, and Colter handed her a box of what looked like the entire contents of a craft store, complete with fake white and blue hydrangeas. For a moment she simply stared at the glittering petals. They were a far cry from the skull that she had just been looking at, and it struck her how, even in moments of peril, there could always be something beautiful just around the corner.

She walked with Rainier toward the office, and after he opened the door for her, made her way into the back and set the box on the table in Whitney's office. "I don't think they have a clue what's going on. Should we tell them?"

Rainier peered out the window of the door as if checking how far behind them they were. "They are going to learn soon enough. Wyatt's there now," he said, gesturing toward the truck.

Glancing outside, Laura could see the evidence bag in Wyatt's hand. Colter's and Whitney's smiles disappeared as they spoke. She couldn't hear their exchange, but from the way Wyatt lifted the bag she had to assume he was telling them what Rainier had feared.

"Should we go out there?" she asked.

He stared out for a long moment. As Wyatt continued to speak, Whitney's face grew more and more stoic and she set the box in her hands down on the hood of the truck.

Rainier turned away and closed the door with barely a click. "No," he said, shaking his head.

He didn't need to explain himself further. After everything that had already happened today, Laura couldn't blame him for turning away from more drama.

"When were they planning on having their wedding?"

Rainier shrugged. "I know my mother said something about them doing it around Christmas, but I don't know when exactly. And now…with everything that's happened while they were gone, I wouldn't be surprised if they called it off."

She nodded, but she thought of the excited look on Whitney's face and the way the two had seemed so invested in something as simple as just their wedding colors. She could only imagine how devastated they would be if they had to cancel it. Yet to go ahead with a party on that scale seemed just wrong—almost as if they were trivializing the family's struggles.

"Maybe if we can get to the bottom of this, it's just another thing that can be made right," she said, her words sounding far more hopeful than she felt. She moved toward the door that led to the yard.

"How is that?" Rainier asked, staring out the window in the door.

"Well, if we can solve the murder, my dad can help us solve the tax thing, and then they wouldn't need to postpone anything. We could turn this into the party your mom always wanted and that they badly need."

Rainier ran his hands over his face as he turned away from the door and pulled down the shade, as if by being unable to see them it would keep him at arm's length from all the issues that came with their return. "Do you always look on the bright side of everything, Laura?" He gave her a serious glance, but her name rolled off his tongue like it had tasted of honey.

Him saying her name made her body clench. "I always try to be positive. It's better that way."

He stepped away from the door and closer to her. His nearness made her skin feel as though an electric current was racing through it, and that if he touched her they would both be at risk of getting hurt. Yet she doubted it was electricity, but rather something rarer—something that resembled love.

"Why?" he asked, and he gave her a look that made the current in her intensify.

"Huh? Why what?" she asked, only half-aware that there were even words coming from her mouth, as all she could think about was the way he smelled of winter air and Irish Spring soap.

"Why are you always so positive? How is it better?" he pressed, but this time his voice was softer, deeper.

"Like attracts like," she said, staring at his lips and the way they were pulled into a sultry grin. "So if I was pessimistic all the time, I'd bring in the results I expected."

"But isn't it better to expect the worst and be happily surprised when the good happens, instead of hoping for the best and constantly being disappointed?"

"If you knew me a little more, you'd know that I'm hardly ever disappointed." As she said the words, she knew they weren't entirely true—her father disappointed her all the time. But by and large most of the other areas of her life were marked by their greatness.

He reached over and cupped her face in his hands. She basked in the warmth of his callused palms against her skin.

"What if I disappoint you?" he asked, moving slightly closer, so close that his breath brushed against her face and warmed her cheek.

He was going to kiss her. She could feel it in his touch and hear it in the lilt of his voice, and though she wanted it, there was a nagging voice in the back of her head that kept telling her how stupid it would be to let him. If he kissed her, the rules of their game would change. Their roles would be altered. Her job would be compromised. Heck, his entire future could be jeopardized.

"You won't," she said as his lips grew nearer to hers, so near that she closed her eyes and readied herself to feel his lips press against hers. "And we… can't," she said, nearly breathless.

But he didn't stop. And she didn't pull away.

His lips met hers. All the desire she had been feeling poured through her, and the only thing she could think about was the glory and excitement of his kiss. The ways his lips moved reminded her of him, the way he walked, the rhythm of his speech and the gentle strength that seemed to characterize him. In a way, it completed him and the way he made her feel. As their mouths moved together, giving and taking as they tasted one another, she could only imagine that having sex would have been even better.

She wrapped her arms around him, running her fingers through his hair. It was softer than she had expected and she rolled it around her fingertips as his kisses moved from her lips to her chin, and finally her neck. She exhaled and it came out as a gentle moan, and at the sound his muscles tensed.

He pressed his body into her as he walked her deeper into the back office until she was backed against the far wall. He moved between her legs, lifting them around his waist as he kissed her neck. He was as hot as his kiss.

"Rainier." She said his name as though it was the last time she'd have the chance to whisper his name. "You… We… Mmm…" She moaned as he met her heat.

"I'll go back to being a good little parolee, I promise. No one has to know."

The nagging voice in the back of her head screamed that those were famous last words that would inevitably come back to bite her, but she pushed the thought to the side. Maybe no one would find out. It wasn't wrong to follow her heart, not when her feelings for Rainier were stronger than anything she had ever felt before. This was right. They were right. And his kiss… Oh, his kiss…

His hands moved down her sides as he held her against the wall. She rolled her hips, letting her body show him exactly how much she wanted this.

He reciprocated, matching her movements with his own. The world around them disappeared and all she could think about was the pulsing need between her thighs and the fulfillment that his body promised.

She was pulled from her reverie when a man cleared his throat.

She opened her eyes to find Merle Fitzgerald standing at the open back door. She pushed against Rainier, who was still kissing her neck. He didn't seem to notice.

"Hey, Rainier," she said, wiggling out of his arms and lowering her feet to the floor.

Merle turned away slightly, giving her a chance to recompose herself. She stepped out of Rainier's arms and readjusted her skirt, then patted her mussed hair.

Rainier turned and, seeing his father standing in the doorway, grabbed a book from the shelf and carefully placed it over himself. "Dad…" He looked at her and mouthed the words *I'm sorry*.

There was no possible way that he could be sorrier than her. The voice in her head had been right. His promise to keep this their little secret and "no one has to know" had already gone out the window.

Rainier ran his hand over his hair, flattening it where she had pushed her fingers through it. "Dad, what are you doing here?" he asked after clearing his throat.

Merle turned toward them. "I just wanted to take a look at the books and see how many reservations we had coming up," he said, motioning toward the computer in the main office area.

Something about his posture and the way he said the words seemed off, almost as if he was lying to them. Yet right now Laura felt hardly capable of judging the situation. After what Merle had just seen, it would be strange if he wasn't just a little bit off.

"Oh, okay," Rainier said. "Can't you look at that on the computer in the house?"

Merle frowned. "Yeah, but well… You know, I thought maybe this had a different schedule than ours. I just wanted to check."

Once again there was something about what he was saying and how he was saying it that made her wonder what Merle was hiding.

"No worries, though. I'll just look into it later," he continued. "By the way, did you hear anything about what your brother found? Looks like Lyle and Steve are wrapping things up back there. I asked them about it, but they wouldn't tell me anything. What do you guys know?" he asked, almost rambling as he spoke.

Something was definitely amiss with Merle, but Laura tried to tell herself that it was just because of the circumstances in which he had found them.

Rainier gave her a questioning look, almost as though he was hearing the same things.

"You'll have to ask Wyatt. He didn't tell us much," Rainier lied.

His father wrung his hands as he walked to the front of the office and peered outside. Wyatt, Colter and Whitney were still standing in the parking lot, talking.

Laura couldn't understand why Rainier had kept the truth from his father, but now wasn't the time to question him.

Merle turned back to them and let the shade fall back in place in the window. "If you hear anything, tell me. I have to know. It can make the difference between the life and death of the ranch."

Chapter Ten

Whitney's eyes were red from the tears she had been shedding for the last hour, after they'd learned of the events that had taken place at the ranch while they were out of town. The entire family was huddled around the dining room table. Even Wyatt was there, holding Gwen's hand. It felt a bit odd to have Laura sitting at his side during a family meeting, but Rainier couldn't deny that something also felt very right about having her there. Everyone had been so welcoming to her, perhaps even more than they had been to him. It was almost as if she was already a member of the family.

He was getting ahead of himself. Just because they'd had one quick make-out session that had been rudely interrupted by his father didn't mean that it was ever going to happen again, nor that it should. He wished it was easier to control himself around her, but every time they were near one another it was as if the world ceased to exist and all the rules and regulations that dictated their behavior were nothing more than suggestions.

He was tempted to reach over and take her hand, to make her feel even more welcome and supported by him, but he resisted the urge. No one in the family needed to know what was going on. Based on his father's reaction, it wouldn't be prudent to tell anyone what was happening between them—it would only put Laura and her job at risk.

"I won't hear of it," Eloise said. "This will all settle down. You know how things go here—there's always something that comes up, some hurdle that we have to overcome. We always find a way. It's what makes us Fitzgeralds. The second we give up and roll over is the second we really lose."

"Mom," Wyatt said, his voice soft and filled with concern, "we need to face the facts. If we can't find a way to get out of paying these taxes, this ranch is going to go up for sale. All the people here and you and Dad—you'll all be without jobs. For once, you need to do what's best for *you*. And I don't think that hosting a wedding right now is even close to being in your best interest."

Whitney and Colter were gripping each other's hands so tightly that Rainier could see the white tendons in the back of Whitney's.

Wyatt looked over to them. "You know I love

you guys, and I want the very best for you," he said, squeezing Gwen's hand. "And your love isn't going anywhere. It's not going to lessen if you wait… I mean, look at me and Gwen. We wanted to get married as quickly as possible, too, but after we discussed it, we knew it wasn't the right time for the family."

Rainier glanced at Laura, trying to gauge her response to Wyatt's proclamation, but her face gave nothing away. He couldn't tell whether she agreed or disagreed. In fact, she'd been silent ever since they'd followed his father out of the office. Maybe she was feeling as conflicted over what had happened as Rainier was.

He wished he could take her out of here and they could just finish what they'd started. Though, admittedly, he would have been almost as happy to finally have a chance to just sit and talk with her. So much of their time together had been spent focused on the world around them, the taxes and the investigation. He wanted to know so much more about her—like if she was a sweets or salty eater, if she liked football, or any sports, for that matter. And he wanted to know more about her family. Maybe her family was more like his than he even realized. Maybe that was why she didn't seem to react to his brother being so protective.

"Wyatt, you're a smart man, and a lot of the time

I think you're right. I've never thought of you as having anything other than a great head on your shoulders," his mother said. "But right now, you're being an idiot. This is about so much more than a wedding. This party could show the world the kind of family we are."

Wyatt leaned back in his chair but kept his mouth shut.

"Think about it," his mother continued. "If we only have a few more weeks at this place, I want them to be the best weeks ever. I don't want our memory of this place, of Dunrovin Ranch, to be destroyed by an evil man…a man with a vendetta. William may win. He may get his way. Bullies sometimes do. Yet he can only win if we quit fighting and give up the things that make us great. Let's have this wedding. Let it be a symbol of our greatness. Even if we lose our home, we can still win, because we will have lived our lives to the fullest and have stuck together."

A tear rolled down Whitney's cheek unchecked. She stood up and, walking around the table, wrapped her arms around Eloise's neck.

Rainier couldn't hear what Whitney was whispering in his mother's ear, but it had to be what they were all thinking…that his mom was an incredible woman. If he became half the person she was, he would consider himself lucky. She always had the right answer. She always had the right perspective. He couldn't imagine a better matriarch.

"Mom, I agree with you," Wyatt said. "But you are forgetting that we are dealing with human remains out there."

Eloise nodded, putting her hands up, shushing his brother. "I know, but whoever those bones belonged to is long gone. They're not going to know whether or not we have a wedding." She gave a slight smile. "I mean, we should have some sort of memorial for him, but it may be months before we even learn who he was. In fact, we may never know. Those remains are the epitome of a cold case. Wyatt, do you really think Lyle and Steve are going to solve this?"

His brother's features tightened, but Rainier couldn't tell if it was because of anger or the fact that their mother was right in assuming the lead investigators on the case were probably not up to the challenge.

Laura looked over at him. She scrunched her face and it made her look cuter than ever. "Think we should go?" she whispered.

She must have thought this was going to lead to a fight. He wondered if this was just a unique set of circumstances, as it was his family that was on the brink of disaster.

He nodded and reached to take her hand, but she drew away from him.

She stood up and he followed suit. "I'm sorry to interrupt," Laura stated, "but I don't think I should be involved with this—it seems like a family matter."

His mother glanced at the two of them, looking as though she wished Rainier would voice his opinion on the matter. Truth be told, he agreed with Laura. Everything about the situation was complicated, but ultimately it was not his decision to make, but Whitney and Colter's.

"I'm sorry, Laura," Eloise said. "I didn't mean to be rude. And I didn't mean to drag you into this. Thank you again for everything you've done for us. Knowing that your father is looking into things is a huge burden off my shoulders."

Laura twitched. "It's an honor to help." She leaned down and gave his mother a quick peck on the cheek.

Eloise reached up and gave her a hug, and as he watched, Rainier could have almost sworn that through déjà vu or something, he'd seen it before—or maybe it had been in a dream. For that was what Laura was to him—something sent to him in a dream, and just like a dream, she wasn't permanent, but would dissolve into nothingness if he tried to hold on. Loving her was futile. They could never be. No matter how badly he wanted to see his dream become a reality.

Rainier grabbed her coat, which she'd hung near the door, and helped her slip it on. He followed her outside to the parking lot, where her car waited. Their footsteps crunched in the inches of freshly fallen snow. It had been snowing almost constantly for the last few hours. Lyle and Steve were smoking cigarettes beside the barn, their backs turned to them. Laura didn't say a single word, and it wasn't until she unlocked her car and opened the driver's-side door that she finally turned around and looked at Rainier.

She nibbled at her bottom lip nervously, as if she wanted to say something to him but didn't know how.

"I know," he said. "I know what you're going to say and you don't need to worry about it. I know what happened back in the ranch's office was a onetime thing and it's not going to happen again, so you don't need to feel bad about it. I'm just going to consider myself lucky that I even got the chance to kiss you."

She glanced over at Lyle and Steve as if checking to make sure they couldn't hear them speaking. "Why don't you get in my car? We can talk in there."

He walked around the side of her black sedan, but before he got in he ran his fingers down the felt reindeer antler that protruded from the top of the door. The thing really was ugly, and he couldn't understand why she would've done something so silly to her car. Yet its tacky cheerfulness made him smile. He liked that she was willing to break from the stereotype and be the one parole officer who wasn't afraid to let a little joy into her life.

He got in and closed the door. This wasn't going to go well, but then he couldn't say anything in his life was going very well at the moment.

She was staring out the windshield as fat snow-flakes fell from the sky and stuck against the glass.

"Do you think it's ever going to stop snowing?" she asked after a long moment.

He wondered if this was her attempt to relieve some of the tension between them, or if she was simply trying to ignore what he had said outside.

"You're from Montana, right?" he replied.

She nodded as she started the car, and cool air poured out at them from the vents.

"Then you know how it is. We can get all four seasons in a single day. Though," he said, glancing over at the thermometer on her dashboard, "at thirty degrees, it may be fair to call today a winter one."

She laughed and the sound made some of the tightness in his chest relax. "I always tell myself that as soon as I retire, I'm moving to Arizona."

"So you want to be a snowbird, eh?"

She smiled. "You can't tell me that thirty and snowing is better than seventy and sunny."

"If you don't like it here, why do you stay?"

Laura looked at him, then reached up and grabbed the steering wheel a bit harder than she had to. "Do you want to get out of here?" she asked, pointing at Lyle and Steve, who were now looking at the car.

"Where do you want to go?"

"I don't know. You hungry?"

They had eaten their fill; his mother had made sure of that when they had all come in, before they'd had their family meeting. Yet if going for another dinner meant that he got to spend more time with her, Rainier was willing to gorge himself.

"Sure, sounds good."

He could tell from the look on her face that Laura had the same thought about his mother's food. But she didn't say anything and, putting her car into gear, made her way out of the parking lot and down the dirt road.

It was awkward as the silence filled the space between them, interrupted only by the occasional jolt as the car hit a rut or frozen cow pie. It wasn't until they reached the main road that she finally turned to him.

"You know, I have a couple of steaks I've been meaning to cook up at my house. I bet you haven't had a good steak in a long time. Interested?"

He couldn't believe that she was asking him back to her place. If this was some attempt for her to show him that they needed to distance themselves from one another, she was failing.

"I'll never turn down a steak. I'm a dude."

She chuckled. "Me, neither, and I'm not a dude.

What does being a dude have to do with anything about enjoying a good steak?" she teased.

"I don't know," he said, trying to match her playful demeanor. "I guess I always thought it was guys who were the steak and potato type."

"Have you dated a lot of women?"

"Are you asking because you think I'm inexperienced, or are you checking on my dating history?"

She laughed. "I'm just doing my due diligence. As your parole officer, it's my duty to be fully informed."

"About my sex life?" he asked with a quirk of a brow.

Either the heat had finally kicked on in the car or he was warmed by embarrassment; either way, he reached up and unzipped the top of his jacket to cool himself off.

"Are you blushing?"

He snorted. "Absolutely not. Must've been all that talk about steak, just me getting hungry."

"Uh-huh, I'm sure," she teased.

He was so confused. She was being flirtatious with him, but it was the last thing he had expected after they had been caught by his father. Had she not thought about what it would mean if their relationship came to light? It was always his belief that women were the brakes in a relationship and men were the gas pedal; but that was not how she was acting, and he didn't know what to make of it, or if he should even bring it up. Maybe this was just her attempt to sweep their kiss under the rug, like it never happened. That made the most sense.

"I think you're confusing hungry with hot," she said.

Maybe he was all kinds of wrong. Clearly, she wasn't pushing him back into the friend zone. Was that why she wanted him to go back to her place—so they could have sex? Oh, to be that lucky.

He fanned himself. "You're right, I guess I am kinda hot, and I don't mean just my looks."

"Oh, my God, I can't believe you just said that. You're ridiculous." She laughed again. "Humble much?"

"Oh, I'm humble, but when you've got a body like mine," he said, running his hands down his abs in a failed attempt to be sexy, "you just gotta flaunt it."

"If that's the only move you've got, I'm gonna turn this car around and take you back home," Laura declared with a giggle.

It would be smarter to have her take him home, of that he had no doubt. But he couldn't walk away from this—regardless of the consequences.

Chapter Eleven

Laura had never considered herself adept at flirting, or at the relationship game for that matter, but she was profoundly proud of herself as she parked her car in her garage. She had done it. She had made her feelings toward him known, and instead of playing some kind of coy game, had just let things be real between her and Rainier.

She walked through the back door of her house just outside of Mystery, Rainier close behind her. The place smelled like cinnamon sticks and pine, thanks to her Christmas tree.

"Wow," Rainier said, walking into her kitchen from the garage. "You are really into Christmas, aren't you?" He glanced over to the window ledge above the sink, which was covered in a variety of snowmen.

She glanced around and, for the first time, noticed the place for what it was—an homage to all things of the season. Every surface had at least one Christmas decoration, from stuffed reindeers to expensive gold-rimmed china.

"It's my favorite season," she said as she walked by her kitchen table and ran her finger along the edge of the gold charger plates she used to decorate the space. "I actually own an online store. I supply handmade Christmas decor to sites like Amazon."

He laughed. "Well, now those reindeer antlers on your car make a little more sense."

"How's that?"

He gave her a sexy half grin, as if he didn't want to fess up to what exactly he was thinking.

"Hey now," she teased, "don't go bashing my antlers. It took me a lot of hours to get those patterns right. Now they are one of my company's best sellers."

"Reindeer antlers for your car?" he asked, sounding a little shocked.

"People love them. Though it seems like the most sales are coming from the South. It's all marketing and targeting your demographic."

He gave her a look that suggested she had just lost her mind.

Laura took off her jacket and hung it on a chair, right over a decoration that made the back of the chair look like Santa's face. She smiled as she thought of what the place must look like to Rainier.

Hopefully, it wasn't a turnoff—like walking into a house full of cats if you didn't love felines.

Though she did have three: Albert, Einstein and Sappho. Sappho always had a habit of running off to Laura's office and hiding atop her bookshelf.

The empowerment she had been feeling started to slip as she thought of all the reasons Rainier wouldn't want to have a relationship with her now that he had more of an idea what her private life looked like. And that was to say nothing about the conflict of interest that came with dating one of her parolees.

A groan escaped her.

"Are you okay?" he asked as he tugged off his jacket and laid it over hers.

"Yeah," she lied.

This had been a stupid idea; she shouldn't have brought him here. She shouldn't have kissed him. They couldn't be alone. If someone else besides his father found out what they were doing, she could lose her job.

At the thought, she realized that deep inside her the thought of being unemployed didn't strike fear; instead, it was just a void. It was almost as if she didn't care, but that was just as idiotic as her bringing him here. She couldn't *not* work. She had bills to pay and a life to manage. Besides, she wanted to make a difference and help people. Not to mention what her father would say if she quit her job. He was the reason she was doing what she did. He had made sure that she had a *real* job, as he called it.

She walked toward the fridge, inadvertently brushing against Rainier as she passed by. That familiar feeling, that charge she felt when they touched, raced through her body. The feeling was so foreign and pleasantly uncomfortable, and the urge to touch him again was undeniable.

Her fingers found his, almost as if they had a mind of their own, and their hands entwined. He brought them up to his lips and gently kissed the back of each of her fingers, taking his time as he did so. His breath was warm as it caressed her skin, mimicking the softness of his lips.

She wanted him.

Stepping closer, she leaned into him, her hips leading her to the place she most desired to be.

"Laura, we have to talk," Rainier said as he stepped back from her and bumped against the wall near the bar. "I don't want to, but—"

"Then let's not talk." She wanted to move to him, but stopped herself. She couldn't be the one to do all the chasing, and she knew he wanted her. His desire was evident in the way he kissed her and the way his body responded.

"No," he said, shaking his head. "And trust me when I say that I don't want to talk about anything other than to tell you all the things I want to do to your body. But I think…after what happened in the ranch office and how close we are to getting found out…"

"Your father won't tell anyone, right?"

"I don't think so. My dad has always been one to respect people's privacy, but I haven't had a chance to talk to him alone to make sure. For all I know, he's going to be angry. I'm sure he's wondering what the hell we are thinking. Just like I am."

"You don't like what we're doing?" She ran her fingers along the edge of her blouse, popping open the top button in her best attempt to be sexy.

"That," he said, moving toward her and taking her hand again, "has been just about the only thing I've been able to think about ever since the moment I met you. But we both have to be careful here. This isn't smart."

"I've always done what is right and what is smart. It's the reason I became a parole officer. But you know what I *really* want to do?" She reached down and slipped her fingers inside the waistband of his jeans.

He brushed a strand of hair behind her ear, his fingertips grazing her earlobe, and instead of letting his hand drop back to his side he moved to her lips.

"What?" he asked, staring at her with such intensity that she swore she could feel herself melting in the heat.

"I want to stop talking. I want to stop thinking and just *feel* for once."

"You need to know that feelings always have a way of getting me into trouble," he said.

"I normally am not one for trouble. I try to play by the rules." She drew his thumb into her mouth as she unbuttoned his pants. "Well, usually."

If this was what it felt like to break the rules, then she could finally understand why people chose to find themselves sitting in her office. Standing there, her fingers tracing the elastic band of his boxer briefs, and knowing that what she was doing was wrong…it was hot. Hotter than anything she could ever have imagined. She could only dream of what it would feel like to have him between her thighs, driving himself inside her.

He lifted her up and she threw her legs around him. "Which way to the bedroom?"

"It's upstairs. First door on the left." She pointed toward the stairs across from the living room. "If you don't want to go that far, there's always the couch." Or the floor, or the wall, or in front of the fireplace… She'd make love to him anywhere.

His body hardened against her as he shifted her higher in his arms.

"The bedroom it is."

Either the man had the willpower of a saint or there was some other reason he wanted to hold off.

From the feel of him, he couldn't have been worried about disappointing her in the bedroom. In fact, she wouldn't be surprised if she'd be well satisfied, if not a little sore in the morning.

"Why wait to go upstairs when we can have fun right here?" she asked, moving against him.

He looked her square in the eyes. "If we are going to do the wrong thing, I'm at least going to do it the right way."

"And the right way is the bedroom? Are you some kind of sexual fundamentalist? You know, the kind that has sex in only one position—missionary style?" If he was as plain as vanilla in the sack, he could put her down right now—she had made a mistake.

He laughed so hard that she shook in his arms. "Oh, baby, you couldn't be more wrong." He buried his face in her blouse as he kissed the skin of her chest, licking along the edges of her bra.

They stumbled as he bumped against the couch, but he didn't take his mouth from her until they reached the bottom of the stairs.

"If you want, you can put me down. I'm perfectly capable of walking."

"I know you are," he said, slowly making his way upward. To his credit, though she knew she was a bit on the heavy side, he didn't make a single sound— and it only made her like him that much more. "But there's something you may not know about me.

When I am with a woman, especially a woman as wonderful as you, I'm going to give the relationship everything I've got."

Her gut tightened. So he thought this was going to turn into a relationship instead of just being a one-night stand. She should've wanted that, she should've been thankful he wasn't like every other guy who just wanted to use her for sex and then move along.

He constantly surprised her as a man, and he was nothing like the other parolees she had worked with. Which only made what the two of them were doing feel less taboo. Rainier wasn't like a normal con, blaming the world or acting like he had done no wrong, or otherwise trying to rationalize his actions. He owned his mistakes.

Why did she have to think about that right now? It wasn't helping the growing wetness between her thighs.

This was her moment…no, their moment, and she had to enjoy. In the morning, everything would be different.

In the morning they would have to go back to their normal roles, even if he didn't know it yet.

They couldn't have a relationship. At least not until one of their situations changed. Yet they could have tonight, one secret night of passion that she could carry in her heart for the rest of time.

As he carried her into the bedroom, she looked

over at her bed and giggled with embarrassment at the pile of Christmas-themed teddy bears atop her holly-accented quilt. If only she had known this was where the day was going to take her, she would have hidden them away and not let this sexy man see what a single woman did when left to her own devices. Not that she was admitting she needed a man's touch around the place, but it would be nice to have someone who was a little bit taller put ornaments on the tree, or to have occasional help putting up a curtain rod. But for the most part, she didn't need a man— not when there was YouTube to teach her how to do things.

"Why are you laughing?" she asked, as he slowly sat her on the bed. "Are you about to say something about my collection of bears?"

He smiled. "We are all allowed a quirk or two. If yours are Christmas stuff and teddy bears, I think that's far better than a woman who collects machetes."

"Is that right? Are you sure you wouldn't be more into a girl with a little bloodlust?" she teased.

"The only girl I want is you."

That look of his, the one that made her want to melt into a puddle, returned. That look, in conjunction with his oh-so-perfect words, made her rethink her stance on a relationship. Maybe they could make it. But now wasn't the time or the place to think about anything other than the way he looked standing in front of her.

He pushed her back gently until she was lying down. Leaning over her, he undid the rest of the buttons on her blouse. He moved to her skirt, and for a moment just stared at it as if it was a Rubik's cube.

"Here, let me help you," she said, reaching down to the zipper on the side.

"No, no, I got it." He bent and ever so gently grabbed the zipper with his teeth and dragged it open, making her heady with lust.

He tugged at the edges of her skirt, pulling it free of her legs and dropping it to the floor. He didn't wait for her to undress him. Instead, as though suddenly in a hurry, he pulled off his pants and yanked his shirt over his head. He threw it behind him, laughing as he moved atop of her.

"Wait," she said, "do you have a condom?"

"Do you?" he asked.

Of course she did, but she wasn't sure she wanted to admit it—or the fact that they could have expired, even though she had never used any. She wiggled out of his embrace to open her nightstand and grab the black box. She checked the expiration date— they were good, and she sighed with relief. Pulling one of the foil-wrapped condoms from the box, she turned back to him.

He wiggled out of his boxers. She had been right;

he was everything she had hoped and assumed him to be.

"Do you want me to put it on?"

He looked a little bit surprised that she offered, making her wonder if he hadn't slept with many women. She liked the idea, as Rainier was definitely a man who would've had his choice in women.

She ripped open the foil and threw it to the floor. Gently, she unfurled the latex down his length. He was hot in her hand, and as she came to the base, he moaned her name and his voice dripped with desire.

She was still wearing her bra and panties, but it didn't stop him. He folded down the cup of her bra down, taking her nipple in his mouth and sucking, hard. It made a wet, popping sound as he released her and moved to the other side. There was something so sensual about the warm, soft feel of his tongue compared to the scratchiness of her lace bra as it rubbed against her skin.

Maybe the man knew what he was doing, after all.

"Please," she begged.

"Mmm," he murmured, not taking his mouth from her.

"Let me feel you."

He made a sound that was half groan and half growl as he pushed her panties to the side and drove himself into her. She cried out as he filled her, heavy and deep. There had never been a better sensation in the history of mankind. There couldn't have been or they would have died from the thrill of ecstasy.

She took hold of his ass—it was stronger and more muscular than she had realized—and as she held him still inside her, her muscles contracted around him. He felt so good.

Laura moaned, though she had meant to find words to tell him what she was feeling…that she wanted more…that she wanted to be his forever.

She moved against him, letting him pound against her again. Harder. Faster. Then he stopped and, rolling her over, picked her up by her hips and set her on all fours. He moved back into her, pressing her face into the bed. The sheets rubbed the skin of her cheek.

"Oh… I'm close," he said, his voice barely above a whisper.

He hadn't needed to warn her, for she was already there.

Chapter Twelve

Rainier hadn't had to do the walk of shame since before he'd gone to prison, and in the years that had passed, it hadn't gotten any easier. He walked quietly up to the front porch of his parents' house. The lights were on inside even though it was early. Ranching hours. He had nearly forgotten.

He glanced toward the barn, where the door stood slightly open and light from within streamed out and lit up the snow.

"Are you okay?" Laura asked from behind him. "Are you sure you want me to go inside with you? I could just go back home. Come back later or something."

He shook his head. By now everyone had to know that he'd gone home with Laura and she hadn't brought him back. Well, until now.

He couldn't help but think that everything about their relationship was a flip on traditional gender roles, but he didn't mind. Actually, it was a turn-on to have an empowered woman taking an interest in him. Especially since she could be doing so much better for herself. She could be with anyone she chose and yet she wanted to be with him—an ex-con.

There was no denying that he wanted to be with her in every way, but now that it had happened, everything had changed between them. Sure, he could pretend that nothing had occurred and they could try to slip back into their assigned roles, but pretending was all it would be. Beneath it all, everything was muddied and conflicted, now that feelings were involved. They had made a mistake in getting involved with each other, but now that it had happened, he didn't want it to end just because it was inconvenient.

As they walked into the house, they found Rainier's father in the living room in front of the fireplace, setting about lighting it for the day. The room was filled with the familiar scents of struck matches and blazing kindling.

As they approached, Merle turned around and gave them an acknowledging smile. "Good morning, you two. Have a good night?" To Rainier's surprise, the awkwardness of the day before had disappeared from his father's demeanor.

"Uh, yeah. How's it going? I see the sheriff's department team is gone. Did they button up their investigation?"

Merle nodded. "Yep, and Wyatt and I finally got the chance to fix the pipe. With any luck the pump will be okay, but with as much as it was running it may have burned out."

Was his dad really talking about piping and how long the pump would last? Maybe his awkwardness had just taken on a new form and had become avoidance.

"Did Wyatt's team find anything else?" Rainier asked.

His father shook his head. "Thankfully, no."

"What do you mean, *thankfully*?" Rainier pressed.

Merle twitched. "Nothing. You know, just that I'm glad they're not still out there tearing through the pasture. At least now we can get back to worrying about more important things, and this can just disappear."

"You don't think finding a body on the property is at all concerning?" Laura asked.

"No, no. You're getting me all wrong. I just mean that there are so many other things we need to worry about. The dead are dead."

Something was definitely up with his father, but Rainier wasn't sure talking about it in front of Laura was a great idea. She seemed to be firmly on their team, but at some point would have to start putting her work first. Last night she hadn't seem to care about her role as his parole officer, but that was in the privacy of her own home and the comfort of his arms. Yet if his father had anything to do with the murder, or whatever had happened to this person whose body they'd found, then it was going to become more than just a simple distinction between ethical and unethical—it would be a question of legal versus illegal.

Merle Fitzgerald wasn't a murderer, and he wasn't the kind of guy who would ever do anything that would put his family in jeopardy—even if it meant putting himself at risk. In fact, selflessness seemed to be the personality trait his parents had most in common. To them it was always family first.

And maybe his father was right, and the last thing they needed to do was dredge up some cold case. On the other hand, whoever this person might be, he was someone's brother, father or son. The victim's family deserved to know what had happened to their loved one—even if it meant they had to go through an even harder time in order to get closure.

"Dad, I hear what you're saying. To some degree, I think you're right, but we have to see this through. It's not going to just disappear. And I'm not assuming anything, but if you know something you aren't telling the police or Wyatt or whomever…you may want to come clean. It's better to do it now than to wait and have it come out later."

"What are you talking about?" Merle's angst sparked in the air.

He had clearly struck a nerve, which meant he must have struck a nerve or touched on a secret his father was trying to hide.

"Why don't we go get some breakfast?" Laura suggested as though she was as uncomfortable with the situation as he was.

"Great idea. I'll cook us some eggs." He looked back at his father, who had turned away and was stoking the fire. "Dad, are you hungry?"

"No," he said in a clipped tone.

Merle Fitzgerald, in addition to his selflessness, was also known for his stoicism and his ability to control his temper. They had been through a lot over the years, and the only time he could remember seeing his father this upset was when Rainier had been kidnapped by his birth mother when he was a child. The day he had been returned, Merle had been yelling at the police, telling them they had to go after the real person responsible—Rainier's father, the one who had put his wife up to it.

Rainier had been young when everything had happened. He could barely remember most of those fateful days, but the one thing he recalled vividly was the way his adoptive father's face had looked… the way the wrinkles had suddenly appeared around his eyes, making him appear much older than he had just days before. Those lines had never disappeared, but simply deepened with age.

And Rainier remembered the phone call they'd received to let them know that his biological mother had been killed. Everyone knew that his birth father had killed her. Yet when it came time to prosecute, the case had fallen apart and the man had never gone to prison. Some people had gone so far as to say his biological father's evasion of justice was due to political corruption, while others cited ineptitude on the part of the police department—but Rainier had called it just plain wrong. His father had deserved to pay for his crimes, and then and there in front of his father, Rainier had vowed to seek revenge.

It was in that moment that he had last seen Merle Fitzgerald look as he did now, with that same expression of deep-seated anger with an edge of fear. And that look, in addition to the way his father was acting, made Rainier's blood run cold. Nothing good could come of it.

Rainier and Laura went into the kitchen and he set about making breakfast, pulling eggs out of the refrigerator and getting the pans ready. He moved automatically, and as he waited for the electric stove to heat up the pan, he realized that in the years he had been gone, nothing in the house had really changed. All the things he had left behind could still be found as they had been when he'd left—every pan was still in the same cupboard, they used the same cups and plates, and even the ingredients in the fridge were nearly the same. It was as if life had been on hold.

None of that mattered. What mattered was his father and what Rainier was going to do about him.

If he turned to his mother, it would only upset her.

Laura stood beside him, cracking the eggs and dropping them into the pan. "What's going on, Rainier?"

"Huh?" he asked as she pulled him from his thoughts.

"With your father. I don't know him that well, but I can tell that something is wrong. Is he going to be okay? Does this have anything to do with us?"

This was such a departure for her, when she had found him with the bone she had followed the requirements of her job and called the police, yet now it seemed that she was putting their relationship first and he loved it. "Do you mind if I just go talk to him for a minute?" he asked. "Could you maybe take over cooking for a bit?"

"Take all the time you need." She nibbled at her bottom lip.

He turned to walk out of the kitchen.

"You know," she said, stopping him, "I could just head back home. I don't want to make things harder for you and your family. I know you have a lot going on."

He should have agreed and let her go, but every time he was around her, she reminded him that he wasn't alone, and of what life could be. The thought of them being apart made a deep, nonsensical loneliness creep through him. If she left, he was sure she would come back, and they could pick up from where they'd been.

It may have been selfish, but he couldn't let her go.

"No, it'll all be okay. I'm sure he's just stressed. I just need to talk to him," he said, forcing himself to smile in a way that he hoped would lighten the mood and wordlessly assure her that everything wasn't as bad as he was thinking.

He walked over to her and gave her a long, hungry kiss. Her lips carried the saltiness of sweat and the flavor made him long to be back there, making love with abandon. He could have lived and died in the moments they had shared, and he would have died a happy man.

She ran her hand down his face as she leaned back from their kiss, and when she looked into his eyes, he was almost certain he could see love in them.

No. She couldn't love him. It had to be just some momentary reaction like his, some desire to bring back the night in each other's arms, and how carefree they had felt in the moment.

She let go of him. "Go. Go talk to your father. He needs you."

She was right, but Rainier couldn't help the thought that his dad wasn't the only one who needed someone.

It had been a long time since Rainier had been in a relationship, and even longer since he'd thought he'd been in love. Maybe this was just their honeymoon phase, when the other could do no wrong, and as soon as their infatuation was over, they would really see each other for who they were. Not that Laura was anything other than what he assumed, but he… he was far from an angel. Over time, if she came to see him for the imperfect person he was, he doubted she would continue to be with him.

Everything would change. Undoubtedly, she would walk away. And he couldn't blame her.

He had made his choices. He had always told himself that he was ready for the consequences and reprisals for the decisions he had made. He had just never considered the possibility of losing her, especially because he hadn't thought he would get her in the first place.

"Go," she said, motioning him out of the kitchen. "I'll make you some eggs when you are done."

He nodded, but as he looked at her, sadness filled him. Perhaps he was just being pessimistic, and his fears of her dismissing him wouldn't be realized. He couldn't make her choices for her, or change the way she was feeling.

As he turned away, she gave his buns a squeeze. "I'll be waiting."

"Hey now," he said with a laugh. "It's only fair if I get to do that to you."

She waved him toward the door. "Turnabout is fair play…in fact, I'd be disappointed if you didn't come back in here and feel me up when you're done."

Her simple action made some of the roiling ball of emotions within him calm. They'd get through this. If they were meant to be together, they would be…

His father was staring into the flames that licked up the logs in the grate. "How did you know?" he asked, turning around as Rainier closed the door to the kitchen with a quiet click.

"Know what?" Rainier inquired, walking over and standing beside him.

"That I'm not telling you something?" Merle looked at him, his eyes reflecting the fire. The effect was unsettling.

"I've known you my whole life, so I'm surprised you'd even have to ask. Wouldn't you be more worried if I didn't know something was wrong with you?" The only thing that truly surprised Rainier was that no one else in the family had seemed to notice the change in Merle, or at least they had failed to mention it. "What's going on, Dad?"

His father ran his hands over his face, and left behind a smudge of ash on his cheek in the process.

That, along with the light in his eyes, made him look as though he was in the middle of hell.

"I thought I'd never be back here again. I feel so stupid. So ashamed. So relieved. So *everything*."

Rainier was shocked by the man's admission. It had been hard to get his father to confess when he had a headache, even. He'd always been a pillar of strength in the family, so to hear him talk about his feelings was even more unsettling than the way he looked.

"Back where, Dad? What do you mean?"

"I… I just never thought I'd have to deal with this mess again. The body… The man's disappearance…"

"You knew about the body?" Rainier couldn't move. He could barely breathe under the weight of his father's words.

Merle fell to his knees in front of the fire and dropped his head in his hands. "I'm so sorry, Rainier."

"Did you…did you kill the man?" The words seemed like grains of sand scraping against his tongue.

No. His father could have never done something so destructive…not when so many people depended on him. He'd never pull the trigger. Rainier had met many convicted murderers in his time behind bars. Even though many of them proclaimed their innocence, there was always something about those who had ended another person's life—a deadness that filled the convict's eyes, as if a piece of them had died along with their victims.

His father had never had that look. He didn't have the eyes of a killer.

"I may as well have," Merle said, his words muffled by his hands.

Rainier didn't understand what he could possibly mean.

"If you didn't pull the trigger, then you are not responsible." He paused. "You didn't pull the trigger, did you?"

His father looked up at him with a jerk. "No. I'd never."

"But?"

"But I knew he…his body…was out there somewhere," he said, waving in the direction of the pastures. "I should have called the police."

Chapter Thirteen

The front door slammed. Laura wasn't sure what she should do—stay in the kitchen and ignore whatever was going on between Rainier and his father, or go and make sure that the two men were all right. She waited for a moment, hoping to hear something, but the only sound was the sizzling of the oil in the pan as she waited to put in another egg.

Certainly things between the two of them couldn't have gone so badly that one had stormed out. Besides, Rainier wouldn't have left her standing alone in his parents' kitchen without so much as letting her know where he was going, or coming to get her before he left. Though he had his issues, he wasn't thoughtless.

Yet if it was his father who had gone, it didn't explain why Rainier wasn't coming to tell her what had happened—not that she needed to know. No, whatever had been said between father and son could stay between them. She was an interloper, an outsider in the tightly woven Fitzgerald clan.

She turned off the stove and removed the pan from the heat.

It was eerily quiet.

Unable to stand it any longer, she opened the kitchen door and looked into the living room. Standing beside the Christmas tree were Merle, Rainier and Wyatt. Wyatt was in his uniform and had his thumbs hooked into the armpits of his bulletproof vest as he stood talking.

He looked over at her and frowned. "Laura, what are you doing here?"

She should have stayed in the kitchen.

"Good morning, Wyatt."

He dropped his hands as he glanced at his brother. "Why is she here?" he asked, his voice cracked with accusation.

"I...I was dropping him off. I was just about to leave," she said, heading toward the front door in hopes that she could get out of there before Wyatt had another chance to interrogate her.

He didn't have to know anything—in fact, he was the last person who needed to know what had gone on between her and Rainier. Though he and his brother had called a tentative truce, if he learned that they were sleeping together she was sure it would all come to a head once again.

"You don't need to go," Rainier said. "Wyatt, you don't have any right to ask about my guest."

"Your *guest*?" Wyatt gave a contemptuous chuckle. "Oh, I see."

"You don't see anything," Rainier said, jumping to intercede. "Why don't you just stop busting my chops and tell us all why you are here, Wyatt?"

"Whatever. To make things clear, Laura, I like you, but whatever you two want to get mixed up in… that's your mistake to make. I just don't want to get wrapped up in your mess."

"Why are you here, Wyatt?" Rainier asked again.

He gave her one last look. "I came here to let you all know that we got our report back from the medical examiner. As we assumed, it was a male. Turns out he was fifty-two years of age, five foot nine, Caucasian, brunette. Cause of death was a gunshot to the head."

"Murder or suicide?" Rainier asked.

Wyatt answered with a cynical smile. "Hard to tell."

"How do you know so much about what the man looked like, based on just a skull and a femur, but can't tell me who pulled the trigger?" Rainier asked.

"Good question," Wyatt said, slapping his brother on the shoulder. "The ME also managed to pull some dental records. They got a match."

Merle walked to the couch and sat down. He

glanced over at her, and there was a look of terror in his eyes. It was so frightening that Laura was tempted to turn away, but she forced herself to stand her ground. She had to be reading him wrong. Merle had nothing to be frightened of…unless…

"The body belonged to Paul Poe." Wyatt gave a long exhalation, like he was working up the courage to finish talking. "Paul was William Poe's father."

Rainier stared at his dad. "You have to be kidding me."

"'Fraid not," Wyatt said. "Their findings were conclusive."

"Have you told William yet?" Laura asked.

Wyatt glanced at her, but the distaste that had marked his gaze now seemed to be gone—as though he had bigger fish to fry than what was happening between her and his brother. For once she was thankful that someone had died. Well, perhaps not thankful, but grateful that the discovery of the identity could cover up what she wished to keep discreet.

"Are you here in a private or professional capacity?" he asked her.

She looked to Rainier, hoping he would supply whatever answer best suited their needs. "I, er…"

"She's here as a friend. Isn't that right, Laura?" Rainier interjected, but the way he said her name made her wonder if they were even that.

"Yes, I'm here as a friend. Why?"

"Then you will keep my little secret?" Wyatt asked.

She nodded.

"Good." He turned slightly to face them all. "Under normal circumstances, I would first have to notify the next of kin—William. However, given the situation, I wanted to tell you all first."

"William is going to be out for blood—even more than he already is," Merle said, his voice worn thin.

"Is there anything we can do…to keep us safe from any kind of reprisal?" Rainier asked, dropping down onto the couch next to his father.

Laura could hardly blame him for needing to sit down. Even her knees were weak at the thought of how William was going to react when he received the news. He was already trying to take the ranch out from under them.

"Wait," she said "With this new break, maybe I can convince my father to take the case."

"What do you mean, *take the case*?" Merle asked. "You said your dad was already working on it."

Laura nibbled at her bottom lip. "That may not have been entirely true… Let's just say he's been a bit resistant. But I didn't want to burden you with that, along with everything else you'd been going through."

"I see." Merle gave a thoughtful nod. "It may be

best if we don't tell Eloise about this. She's been so thankful to your father. She thought he would wrap this all up."

"And he may, but it's going to take a little more convincing to get him to come to our side with this."

"Do you really think he will? We both know that your father is William Poe's friend." Wyatt crossed his arms over his chest.

She shook her head, and raised her hands in an attempt to stop him from getting ahead of himself. "Wyatt, you of all people should know how politics work. My father and William are civil—they have done favors for each other in the past. That doesn't mean they are friends."

"Why would your dad want to take on this case?" Wyatt asked.

The truth was she didn't know. All she could do was hope that her father would see the desperation in her eyes and be unable to refuse her when she begged for help again. At least this time when she talked to him she would have information.

Her father was a hard-edged man, and controlling, but maybe she could convince him that he had been wrong—and that the Fitzgeralds were a family worth saving.

Things with his father couldn't be left as they were. Rainier had so many questions, and yet now he wasn't sure that he could get him alone to hear the answers he so desperately needed.

Merle had been so vague. What had he meant, the man had just *disappeared*? Did he think Paul Poe had left of his own free will—or something else? Something far more sinister? His father had seemed convinced that he was complicit in the man's death, but why? There had to be more to the story than what he had told him.

Yet such was life, and Rainier suddenly found himself deep in the situation at hand—dealing with the revelation that the man in question was William's father. The one thing Merle had made clear was that William would be out to take the Fitzgeralds down. And the only thing he could do right now was prepare for war.

War. The word rattled through him. He would have to do everything in his power to keep his family safe—and Laura, too. What if Poe went after her? He certainly had enough power to get her fired, or at least mess with her career. Hopefully, he wouldn't think to target her. There was no way for him to know about their relationship. Now more than ever it was vital that they kept their feelings under wraps.

Rainier glanced over at Laura, who was putting on her boots. Even though the tension in the room seemed so immense that it pressed against him like some invisible hand, he couldn't look away from her.

She was so beautiful. If William saw them together, Rainier would have to do everything in his power not to give his attraction to her away. It would be one of the most challenging things he would ever have to do.

He walked over to her and lifted her coat so she could slip her arms in the sleeves.

"Thank you," she said, giving him a tired smile.

His father and Wyatt exchanged glances, but he pretended not to notice. They could think what they wanted, just so long as William never found out.

Hopefully, Rainier's family was still as strong as it had once been, and when push came to shove they would come together instead of turn on one another. Yet the only way that would happen was if Wyatt was truly over his animosity toward him, and Rainier wasn't sure. Wyatt had said he liked Laura, but he clearly didn't approve of her choices.

Rainier opened his mouth, hoping that he would think of the right things to say to convince his brother that he wasn't making the wrong choice by following his heart when it came to Laura, but no words came out. It could be he himself wasn't sure that what he was doing was right, putting her in danger the way he was.

No, they were both adults. They had both made the decision to fall for one another—and they both knew what was at stake. Besides, he couldn't deny the way he felt when he was near her, or the way he could imagine their future—two small children, white picket fence, him working at the ranch and her following her dreams of making Christmas special for the world.

Love wasn't something that could be controlled or denied. It was one of those mysterious forces that was greater than them, greater than any sort of argument they could make against it. It was just... meant to be, regardless of the obstacles that stood in their way.

At least for him.

Laura stepped away from him as she grabbed her purse. "I hope my father is going to be okay with us just dropping in. He may be busy when we get there."

She couldn't have known what Rainier was thinking or feeling, but the way she had moved away and seemed a bit distracted made him worry. God, he was so confused. He didn't remember love being this hard. Fighting for survival in prison was easier than dealing with feelings.

Though it was a bit of a drive to her father's law office, thanks to her company, it didn't feel as though it took very long.

When they arrived, there was a young couple seated in the lobby, the man looking distant, as though consumed by thoughts of what they would face once they went in to see their lawyer. Rainier couldn't help but wonder what they were there for, and if he looked like them—full of concern, and half ready to run.

He looked over at his dad as he walked into the lobby, having just arrived. Even though he was adopted, with the exception of the gray hair at his temples and the collection of wrinkles on his face, they mirrored each other.

He'd do anything to make that look on Merle's face disappear.

Laura walked over to the secretary's desk. "I was hoping to see my father. We don't have an appointment, but I thought he could squeeze us in."

The secretary smiled. "I'll let him know you're here, and see what we can do. If you'd like, please take a seat."

As Laura turned back to Rainier he noticed that she, too, was wearing that look of concern. He couldn't blame her. The last time they'd been in this place, his family had been on the losing side and her father hadn't been afraid to let her know exactly what he thought about the case. Hopefully, they had done enough to convince him that they had a case worth taking. If nothing else, maybe he could give them a few answers or suggest a direction they could take to make things right.

The secretary made a quick call, and within a matter of seconds, Mr. Blade was standing in front of them. Rainier had never seen the lawyer before, but even so, he would have known he was Laura's father. They had the same aquiline nose and the same haunted blue eyes. Unlike his daughter, however, the man wore a dour expression, and as he looked at them, Rainier was certain he saw a look of disdain flash over his features.

"Why don't you all step into my office?" Mr. Blade said, waving them down the hallway. He glanced at the couple sitting in the lobby and his expression darkened.

The way he looked at them reminded Rainier of the day he'd gone to trial for his birth father's assault. The prosecutor had worn that same expression, as if no matter what he said or did, the man knew he was guilty as sin.

Rainier followed the others along the hall and into the office.

When he'd been in prison, he'd promised himself that he would never find himself sitting across from another attorney like that, one with hate in his eyes, and yet here he was.

Everything about the lawyer's office, from the mahogany desk to the books that lined the walls, and even the leather chairs, screamed power and prestige. It was no wonder that this man and William Poe were connected; from what Rainier could make out about the guy, they were both consumed by image and politics.

Mr. Blade closed his office door.

Laura didn't wait for her father to speak. "Dad, I don't know if you heard the latest development in the case with Dunrovin." Her hands were shaking, and as she spoke, she balled them in her lap in what was likely an attempt to get them under control.

"What development?" Mr. Blade asked, walking around the side of his desk and sitting down in his leather chair. He motioned for the three of them to take a seat.

Rainier sat between his father and Laura. From where they were, they had to look up slightly, probably some psychological maneuver on the lawyer's part to remind them that he was the one controlling everything that went on in this office.

"We were made aware that the remains discovered on the property were those of Paul Poe. William's father," Laura said.

Merle twitched.

"My family and I are in desperate need of legal counsel, sir," Rainier said, hoping that would take some of the pressure off Laura.

The man nodded. "After Laura was here last time, I had my people do a little digging. So far we haven't found much, but I can tell you that there is a way you can work with the state and the Department of Revenue and create a payment plan that could help you pay your back taxes."

Merle leaned forward and put his hands on the

edge of Blade's desk. "This isn't just about what we owe—this is about justice. You, me and everyone involved here knows that this isn't really about taxes or money. This is about William Poe's desire to destroy me and my family. If you don't see that, you are just as bad as he is."

Though Rainier agreed with his father's sentiment, attacking the man who was possibly going to help them seemed like the wrong approach.

"What my dad means to say, Mr. Blade, is that we are truly grateful you are looking into things. It is appreciated," he said, nodding to Merle in hopes that he would get the message that he needed to keep his temper under control. "We would like to move forward with figuring out a payment plan. However, we would also like to get to the bottom of this thing with Poe. Are you willing to take this on?"

Mr. Blade gave him an approving smile. "I can see you learned some things while you were away."

The man's words grated, but Rainier wasn't sure they had been meant as a jab.

"Dad," Laura said, affronted.

Mr. Blade waved her off. "I'm just commenting that he has moved past his crimes. A man should be proud when he can learn and move forward from his mistakes. It takes great strength to make a blight on a record into something more positive."

She sank back in her chair, but mouthed the words

I'm sorry to Rainier. He gave her an acknowledging tip of the head, but she hadn't needed to apologize for her father—he felt the same way. All he could do was move forward from his past and try not to fall into the trap of resentment and anger it could have generated.

"Thank you, Mr. Blade." He wanted to reach over and comfort Laura, but held himself back. "Now, about my family…"

The attorney stared at him for a long moment as if weighing his options. Tenting his fingers in front of him, he tapped his chin. "This case is going to take a lot of man hours. It could get quite expensive."

Of course his next concern would be their ability to pay.

"Dad, I'll help them," Laura said.

Mr. Blade's mouth gaped open for a moment. "Laura—"

"No," Merle said, interrupting. "We don't take charity. Mr. Blade, regardless of the outcome, we will pay you and your staff for your time. But we want to win. We have to bring William Poe to his knees. I don't want him to use his prestige to go after another family like ours ever again. He cannot be allowed to think his power is absolute."

"As Lord Acton said, 'Power tends to corrupt, and absolute power corrupts absolutely.'" Mr. Blade sent them a sly smile. "If his guilt is as abundant as his hubris, I believe that we may just have a case."

Chapter Fourteen

The next morning it was as if a renewed sense of freedom had taken over the house. From the scent of frying bacon and the sound of women's laughter coming from the kitchen, Rainier guessed everyone was up and busy.

As he made his way down the hallway, he stared at the couch where Laura had spent the night after the long drive back to the ranch. He would be lying if he said he hadn't thought about her out there and wishing she would have come to his bedroom in the night. Several times he had nearly gotten up to go and get her, but he'd decided against it. If she hadn't wanted to spend the night in his arms, then that was her choice.

He peeked into the kitchen, where his mother, Gwen and Whitney were chopping and stirring. Laura stood at the stove. She was fresh-faced, her blond hair hanging long around her shoulders, and she was wearing a sweatshirt complete with an iron-on calico cat. It must have been one of his mother's, and the thought was even more unsettling than the sweatshirt itself. Though, admittedly, Laura would have been cute in anything she chose to wear—even if it was feline inspired.

"Good morning, ladies," Rainier said, winking at Laura as she looked up from frying bacon. "You all need any help in here?"

"Good morning, sunshine." His mother pointed to the gray, cloud-filled dawn outside. "Isn't it a wonderful day? They said it's going to get up to the high teens today."

If he could name a day that wasn't particularly glorious, it was one in which they had to worry about freezing their fingertips off.

"Waylon called. He and the girls are going to be here sometime today." Eloise bustled across the kitchen, grabbing the loaf of bread and putting two slices into the toaster. "I can't wait to see little Winnie. I know it's only been a week or so, but the place has been so quiet without my little sweet pea around. You know, she's going to be turning three this spring. How time flies!"

From his mother's letters, he had heard much about the little girl that his brother Waylon had only just found out was his. From what Eloise had written, Waylon's ex-wife, Alli, had kept the secret of who

Winnie's father was from Waylon in hopes that he could live his life and find a passion that didn't revolve around the ranch. But Rainier saw it for what it really was—his family's unparalleled ability to keep even the biggest of secrets.

He thought back to his father's revelation. From the way he spoke, he and his mother had learned about Paul around the time they were adopting Rainier and his brothers—starting twenty-five years ago. It was incredible to think that they could have known about a man's body buried on their property for twenty-five years and never mentioned it.

However, Rainier could have it wrong. His father hadn't come right out and said that they knew Paul Poe was dead—rather that he had disappeared. But then, with all Merle's talk about pulling the trigger... he had to have known Paul Poe had been killed. Which meant it was possible that he knew who had pulled the trigger and why.

Rainier had to talk to his dad. Today. He had to get to the bottom of this. This was one secret that was just too big to let lie. It impacted them all.

"What's the matter, sunshine?" his mother asked. "You seem awful quiet. Aren't you excited about everyone being here for the holidays? And that's to say nothing about Ms. Laura and what she did for our family." She gave Laura a brilliant smile.

"It was the least I could do. I only want the best for you all," she said, sending him a longing glance.

He was right, it did impact them all—including Laura. And for her well-being, maybe it would be better for him to let his father's secret lie dormant. If Mr. Blade learned that they were all keeping secrets, ones that put his daughter at risk, he would undoubtedly drop their case. They could hire another attorney, but then they would be starting over at square one—and time was quickly running out. Not to mention what her father might say to her for getting involved with his family. Judging by their interaction yesterday, her relationship with her dad was nothing like what he had with Merle. Everything between the lawyer and his daughter was tense and wrapped up in what he could only assume was years of hurt feelings.

"Why don't you and Laura go check on the horses? We can handle things in here, can't we, ladies?" his mother said as she took the spatula from Laura. "We'll eat as soon as your father and brothers come around, but you two can eat whenever you please, once it's ready. For now, just go out and enjoy the fresh morning air."

This was by far the happiest he had seen his mother since he had gotten home, and from the way excitement seemed to radiate from her, he could tell it had been a long, long time since she had felt this carefree. It was as if a blanket of worry had been lifted from her, a shroud that had been in place for years.

He hadn't spent any real time in the barns since he had gotten home, and he couldn't wait. Like the rest of his family, he'd grown up riding, roping and enjoying the lifestyle to which he had been introduced as a child. He had missed the feel of a horse's gait and the scents of hay and sweat. Not only could he finally get back in touch with a part of him that had been missing for the last few years, but now he also had someone to share it with.

They each grabbed a coat and slipped it on before they made their way out to the barn. A black mare stood in her stall, looking out at them as they entered. The animal took in a long breath, taking in their scents and, not recognizing them, gave a high-pitched whinny.

"Looks like I'm going to have to introduce myself to my mother's other children," he said with a laugh. "You spend a lot of time around horses?"

Laura shook her head. "I wanted riding lessons and I begged my mother and father to get me some when I was younger, but my father always thought they were too dangerous. One of his attorney friends had a case where a young girl died after a horse rolled on her on the way back to the barn. It ended up costing the man's client hundreds of thousands of dollars to settle with the family."

From the way she spoke, Rainier wondered if her father had cared more about the girl or the legal case that had come from the tragedy.

"From what I can get, you and your dad aren't very close, are you?"

"We talk a lot. He's always been really involved in my life and my choices. He always wanted the best for me."

"Do you mean *involved* or in control?"

She grabbed a handful of pellets from a galvanized bucket and made her way over to the mare. The horse smacked her lips as she chomped on the treat.

"You don't have to answer me if you don't want," he said, knowing he had pushed her too far in asking her about something that clearly made her uncomfortable.

"No, you're not wrong," she said, but her voice was filled with indecision, as if she wasn't sure whether or not she should speak about this. "My father is not like your dad. He's always been the kind of guy who finds comfort in routine. Even when I was a child everything we did was on a schedule. To this day my family sits down for dinner at six thirty on the nose. Once, I was playing high school volleyball and practice ran late. My parents waited for me until I got home. My sisters were so angry."

"Why were they upset?" he asked.

"We were expected to be home on time at all costs. According to my parents and my sisters, I should have left my practice in order to be home for dinner. They felt it wasn't my coach's fault, but mine because I didn't put the family first."

Her story reminded him of being behind bars and what had been expected of him. He had been forced to live by just as restrictive and regimented a routine as she was describing from her childhood. Which made him wonder if he wasn't the only one who had been living in a prison, even if his prison was of a different kind.

"Are you close with your sisters?"

She shrugged. "My eldest sister went to law school and is practicing family law in LA. My other one went to med school and is now an ob-gyn at Kaiser Permanente in Baltimore. To say the least, I'm the black sheep. To my father I've been nothing but a source of disappointment. He thinks I should have gone to law school or med school or some Ivy League college, and he has made it a point to tell me more than once that he thinks I've wasted my life."

"By being a parole officer?"

She ran her hand down the mare's cheek. The horse nudged her hand, urging her to feed her another pellet. "I never wanted to become a parole officer. My father got me this job." She said it like it was a touchy subject.

"Do you like it?"

She looked over at him and smiled. "There are parts of it that I love."

He stared at her. Had she meant that she loved him?

"But there are definitely days I wish I hadn't let my father push me into this line of work. Most parolees and ex-cons aren't anything like you. So many are truly evil. I read their files and I see the things that they've done, and I know that out in the civilian world they're probably going to become repeat offenders. It's so disheartening."

"You don't think that some of them can be rehabilitated?" The question was more self-centered than he had intended.

"Like I said, I'm not talking about you, Rainier. I don't know what happened between you and your biological father, but I can tell just by being around you that you are not like many of the convicts I work with. Some of these men are capable of killing and thinking nothing of it. They don't feel things like most people do—don't have remorse for the mistakes they made."

He didn't know if he agreed with her. "I heard so many stories when I was inside. You know the one thing they all had in common?"

She shook her head.

"All the men I knew felt like they had been unjustly persecuted. I never heard one man say, 'I got what I deserved.' Most of them felt like victims."

"Is that how you felt about what you did?"

"You may hate me for this, but I might have more in common with those ex-cons than you think." He walked over and took her shoulders, then turned her to face him. "I don't regret what I did. I don't regret hitting that man. To this day, I know that if I was put in a similar situation I would act the same way. My father was evil."

"So you don't think you're guilty? You think you're the victim?" All the softness in her face disappeared and there were tears welling in her eyes.

"As an adult, I'm not a victim. I knew what I was doing when I chose to act the way I did. I deserved to be sentenced like I was. But as a child…as *that* man's child…I was victimized."

She stepped closer and wrapped her arms around his middle, pressing her body against his. Her hair smelled of lavender and sage.

"I…I don't know what to say, Rainier. 'I'm sorry' just doesn't feel right, like it's somehow not enough to make up for all the things I assume you must have gone through." She looked up at him. "Do you want to tell me about it?"

He didn't want to talk about it. In fact, he never

really wanted to talk about his biological parents with anyone. They were like the demons that lived inside his head and, though it was illogical, he was afraid if he opened up and told her about them, they would haunt her, as well. But if she was really going to be a part of his life, she needed to know about his past—everything about his past, and not just the part from police reports.

"The night my father and I got into a fight...it was just the climax of all that came before. He and I had no business ever being in the same room, but yet... there he was, standing like a cock in a henhouse, smack-dab in the middle of the old bar downtown."

"Yeah, I heard about what happened." She nodded. "Was your father from Mystery?"

"After my mother died, my father wasn't really from anywhere. From what I heard, after her murder, he just hit the road and started traveling around the country like a nomad. His friends told me it was because he was lonely, but I know the truth—he was afraid that if he stayed in any one place too long, the community would figure out what kind of person he really was and work to prove that he had a role in my biological mother's death. It was his way of running from the law."

She frowned. "You told me he was an evil man, but what did your father do?"

The mare nickered from her stall and, stretching her neck out, gave Laura a nudge for another pellet.

"You better feed her or she's likely to bite." Rainier gave her a weak smile as he let her go so she could return to the horse.

He didn't want to release her, but he was starting to sweat as he thought about all the things his dad had done to him in the years that he had lived with his biological parents. He glanced down at his arm, even though the burns his father had given him were covered by his coat sleeve.

Laura looked at him as if she knew he was trying to emotionally distance himself, but thankfully, she didn't point it out. Getting close to someone meant that he had to trust them, and trust was one thing he had always fallen short on—especially when his cellmate was just as likely to shank him in the night as he was to give him a piece of gum.

She held out her hand for the mare to take another pellet. "You said your mother was murdered?"

A flicker of anger moved through him. "Yeah, she died about a year after I came to live with the Fitzgeralds."

"How did you come to live with them?"

"My mother and father, they had always had their share of problems, but it all came to a head when I was about three. From what I know, we were coming back from Washington and my parents were pulled over by the highway patrol. My mother was driving."

Laura didn't look at him, and he was a bit relieved. It made telling her his truth that much easier.

"They searched the car. I was sitting in the back seat, asleep in the sun." As he spoke, he could remember the feel of the heat on his skin, but most everything else from that time was a blur. "They found several bags of meth and a collection of drug paraphernalia. From what I could make out from the police report, my mother and father had been using all day."

Laura shook her head as she ran her hand over the mare's forehead. "What happened?"

"I was picked up by Children's Protection Services and they were arrested. From there, I was introduced to the Fitzgeralds. At that time, they were fostering kids and had already adopted Wyatt. They were in the process of adopting Waylon and Colter, too."

"Do you remember coming to the ranch?"

"I remember thinking that it was the most magical place on earth. You know…my version of Disneyland."

She smiled, but there was a deep sadness to it.

"No, really," he said, feeling like he needed to clarify. "It was amazing. Everything before in my life was just darkness, hunger and pain." He took off his coat. "The only real memory I have of my father from when I was very young was when he gave me these." He rolled up the sleeve of his plaid shirt so she could see the little puckered circles that were littered on the inside of his forearm. "He used to love to put his smokes out on me. Thought it was real funny."

She gasped as she took her arm in her hands. Her skin was oily from the horse, but even so her touch felt good.

"Who would do this to a child?" she asked, her fingers running over the scars.

"Like I said, my father was a cruel man. And what he did to me…it was nothing in comparison to what he ended up doing to my mother when he murdered her."

Laura leaned down and kissed the circles near the crook of his elbow. They were hard to see and she wouldn't have noticed them if he hadn't pointed them out and told her what they were. She laid her cheek to his skin and closed her eyes, as if she wanted to take away the pain he had experienced when he was a child. "Why didn't you show me these the other night?"

He shrugged, pulling his arm out of her grasp, then rolled his sleeve back down to cover his scars. Showing them to her made him feel more vulnerable than if he had been standing there naked for the whole world to see. Though she wasn't the kind of woman who would ever turn the truth against him, he couldn't get over the shame and embarrassment that filled him.

"This isn't something I have ever really talked about. I think you're the only person, other than my parents and brothers, who knows the truth about those scars."

Her fingers trembled as she reached toward him. "Thank you. I…I hope you know you can always tell me anything."

Her phone buzzed from her back pocket, reminding him that they weren't alone in the world and, no matter how badly he wanted to forget what stood between them, she had the power to put him behind bars if this all went wrong. If she was like the people in his past, she would use what he told her to explain to a judge why she believed he should be sent back to prison. She could tell them that he was too broken, too risky to be set free.

"Do you need to answer the phone?" he asked, but as he spoke even he could hear the harsh edge in his voice.

"Whoever and whatever it is, it can wait." She reached over and clasped his fingers.

He hesitated for a moment, not wanting to open himself up any more, even if that meant just holding her hand.

"Tell me…what happened to your mom?" There

was a kindness in her voice that calmed the fears bubbling inside him.

She wouldn't hurt him—not like his biological parents had.

"When my mother was released from the county jail, she came to find me. At that time, they were living in the next town over and word had made its way through the gossip mill that CPS had placed me at Dunrovin. It was only a matter of days before she showed up here. I was playing with Waylon out in the pasture when she took me."

"Your mother kidnapped you from foster care?"

"Yeah, but the police found me, returned me to the Fitzgeralds, and I've been here ever since—except when I was locked away." He squeezed her hand. "I later learned that when my biological father found out that my mother had kidnapped me, he waited for her to post bond, and when she got out, he was waiting and he put a bullet in her head."

"He…he *shot* your mother? Why would he want to kill your mother for trying to get you back?"

"From what I know, he thought she was stealing me to get me away from him. He thought there was still a chance that I would come back to them."

"So he killed her because he thought she was stealing you from him?"

He shrugged. "Drugs do strange things to the human brain—paranoia among the top of them. And who knows, maybe it was just an excuse to kill the one person who knew the real him."

"How did he not get sent to prison?"

"When the police arrested him, there was no gun on scene. Though he hadn't admitted to killing her, they knew that he was behind it, and in an effort to speed everything up, they planted a gun on him. During the trial it all came out, and he got off."

Laura opened her mouth to speak, but closed it before any words came out; instead she just stood there, shaking her head.

He didn't know what else to say, either.

Finally, she looked up at him. "I get it. I get why you would want to strike that man."

"Like I said, I have no regrets. I made no mistake in hitting him…but if I'd have known he was at that bar and would have been emotionally prepared to see him, I think I would have killed him. That way no one else in the world would ever have to suffer because of that man."

As HIS PAROLE OFFICER, Laura was required to report Rainier for what he had just said. He clearly wanted to kill his father. Yet as his friend and lover, she couldn't deny that there was legitimate reasoning behind his feelings. If she had been in his shoes, she doubted she would have felt any different. In fact, just seeing and feeling the scars on his arms made her want to find his father and put a bullet in his head herself.

Children deserved to be protected above all else. Sure, wounds inflicted on the skin would heal, but injuries inflicted on the heart would never completely mend. The darkness she had noticed in Rainier's eyes made sense now. He was a child who had spent his days in blackness, and something like that left a mark.

No matter what either one of them did, there would be no going back in time and getting justice for all those his father had hurt, or saving the little boy Rainier had once been. There was only saving the man he was now. And though she wasn't the only one who had a role in Rainier's welfare, she was one of the only people who could help him avoid going down a path that mimicked his father's.

"Rainier, you're right in hating him. I hate him, too, but murdering him isn't the answer. Murder is never the answer. Taking a life changes a person forever, even if it's self-defense. Each time you close your eyes all you'll be able to think about is the choice you made. And when all you see is death, you can't come back to a world in which life and happiness take center stage."

"So basically you're saying that I shouldn't kill because it will give me PTSD?" he asked.

"Don't look at me like that. PTSD is serious. Taking a life is serious."

"I know they are serious. That's not what I meant," he said, raising his hands in supplication. "It's just that it doesn't seem like enough of a reason not to take down a murderer. Don't you think he should have to pay for his crimes?"

"Just because he didn't go to jail doesn't mean that he isn't paying for his crimes. Unless he's some kind of sociopath, I'm sure he is haunted by your mother's death. He has to live with what he has done. And I'm sure at one time, even with all their problems, he probably loved your mom. Which has to make what he did all that much harder."

"You are assuming my father isn't a sociopath." He gave a derisive chuckle. "But you don't know him like I do."

"I may not know him, but I do know you. And I know that you don't want to be anything like him. And if you killed him, you would be doing exactly what he did to your mother. You'd become like him." The words tasted like salt water in her mouth and they burned as she said them.

He cringed as though they had burned him, as well.

"I just want what is best for you, both as your parole officer and as your friend." She wanted to reach over and hold him, but she resisted the urge.

"You deserve to be loved and to have a life filled with everything you want. If you throw it all away in an attempt to sate your anger and your need for revenge, you are only going to hurt yourself in the end. Sometimes, Rainier, the best thing you can do is just let things go."

He looked at her. "Letting go is the smartest thing…but you and I both know how hard it can be to walk away when feelings are involved, good or bad."

He had to be talking about their relationship. Yes, they should have walked away, but it already seemed as if that option was too far out of reach. They had taken things to the point of no return and there was no going back to a time when they could simply let go. Not now.

But this wasn't really about them. This was about his father, his choices and his future.

There was a roar of an engine from the parking lot and the spray of gravel as a car must have come to a stop.

"Do you think that's Waylon and Christina?" Rainier asked, tilting his chin in the direction of the noise. From his tone, she could tell that he was relieved that he could hide from any more talk of feelings and the duality of right and wrong.

Admittedly, she was just as thankful for the interruption, for whenever they started talking about serious things it seemed they always took one step closer to deciding to give up on their feelings. And letting herself feel all she did for Rainier was the first decision she had really made in following her heart and breaking away from what everyone else thought was right or wrong.

She walked with Rainier to the barn door just as a car door slammed in the parking lot.

Looking out, she gasped.

Standing there in the red and green glow of the Christmas lights was William Poe. His normally pristine suit was fraught with wrinkles and his hair was disheveled. He looked over at them and, when he saw them, curled his lips in a punishing smile.

"Rainier Fitzgerald." He said the name like it was a curse. "You are a goddamn murderer. It's time you and your people paid."

Chapter Fifteen

Rainier sauntered out to meet his family's enemy head-on. Opening and closing his fists, he found the rhythmic motion both invigorated and frightened him. William Poe was a foolish man to think he could come here and talk to him that way.

"William, before you say one more thing you're going to regret, you should put your ass back in that car and drive away," Rainier said between gritted teeth.

Laura grabbed him by the wrist and tried to hold him back as he neared the tax appraiser, but he pulled out of her grip. She couldn't stop whatever was about to happen, and neither could he. There were moments in life in which things came to a head, and this was one of them.

William laughed as he looked down at Laura's hand and then back up at him. "You have no right to tell me what or what not to do. In fact, if you were smart, you would listen to your little handler and stay where you are."

"Ha," Rainier said with a snort. "So you're afraid. Good. You should be."

William pulled at the edge of his wrinkled suit jacket in a feeble attempt to straighten it, as though the action could give him a more dignified air. "I have no need to be afraid of you. You are just like the rest of your family—worthless."

Rainier ground his teeth together so hard that they squeaked.

"Rainier, you should just go inside. William is here for a fight." Laura rushed in front of him and put her hands up. "Do I need to remind you of what we were just talking about?"

Walking away was easier when a crazed man wasn't standing in his driveway slandering his family.

"I'm sure Mr. Poe isn't stupid enough to come here for a fight. Or are you, William?" He gave him a warning glance.

"I'm here to set things right. Is your brother Wyatt here?"

The door of the ranch house opened with an ominous screech and his father came walking out, followed by his brother.

"What do you want with me, William?" Wyatt asked. His hair was matted on one side of his head and there was a line on his cheek from where he had just been lying on his pillow, but he was wearing his uniform. Finding William there must have been one hell of a thing for his brother to wake up to.

"Did you really think you could get away with not telling me the body you and your family found on the ranch belonged to my father?" William asked.

Merle and Wyatt both stopped at the edge of the porch, and Wyatt leaned against the railing. For a moment he didn't answer William, but stared at him like he wished he would disappear.

"William, I think you've made a mistake in coming here."

"So you don't deny that you tried to hide my father's death from me?" William took a few steps toward Wyatt, then stopped and looked back at Rainier as though trying to decide whether or not he was a threat if he turned his back to him.

Maybe he wasn't as stupid as he looked.

"I wasn't trying to hide anything, William. I had every intention of notifying you today of your father's passing."

"And yet you were telling the rest of the world about it yesterday?"

Rainier jerked as he looked over at his brother. The only people who knew about the body being Paul's were family members, Laura and her father. Had Wyatt told other people on the force, or had someone else leaked the information before Wyatt could tell William?

"Don't talk about things you don't know or understand, William. It will only lead you deeper into trouble," Wyatt said.

"I'm hardly the one in trouble here." William laughed. "In addition to my father's mysterious death, do I need to remind you about your taxes?"

"We have that figured out," Laura said. "We're going to get the family on a payment plan…so whatever it was that you were hoping to accomplish by undermining this family, you are going to have to try a lot harder."

William sneered at her. "So I've heard. But if you think that the Fitzgeralds are going to be able to get their payments figured out before the deadline, then you are wrong."

Laura's eyes widened with shock and anger.

"What in the hell are you talking about?" Merle asked.

"Do I need to spell it out for you, you dumb redneck?" William asked, smoothing down his hair. "No matter what you and your family try to do to save this little ranch from falling into the hands of the county isn't going to work. It's too late."

"We know you're behind all this, William, and as soon as we can prove it, we are going to have you fired. You are going to be in far more danger than we are," Merle said. But his voice wasn't filled with the same conviction that was in his words.

William leaned against his car. "You don't have a clue what you are talking about. Maybe if you could take your head out of your ass, you would see that your world is going to crash down upon you and your family. I will make sure of it, but that doesn't mean I'm the one at fault. If you want to know who is really responsible for all this, you should look in the mirror."

Merle turned around and walked into the house, slamming the door behind him. Wyatt gave Rainier a questioning glance, but he couldn't have told his brother what William was talking about or what he seemed to be accusing their father of, because he didn't have a clue.

"You need to get your ass out of here and off this property. Or I will arrest you for trespassing," Wyatt said.

"You enjoy that power and authority while you can, Wyatt, because I'm coming for your job next."

"I'm not afraid of you, William. You are nothing but an overinflated, egomaniacal prick who thinks he can control and manipulate everyone around him into giving him what he wants."

William straightened up and walked toward Wyatt.

"Don't you dare take one more step toward my

brother," Rainier said, moving around Laura and making his way over to the man.

William turned. He looked him up and down as if sizing him up and then lifted his nose in the air. "I don't know who in the hell you think you are, Rainier Fitzgerald."

"I'm the man who is going to stop you. I've heard all about you."

"Oh, what have you heard? Aside from your brother's colorful analysis of my character?"

"I know that you think you can control women, that they are nothing more than playthings to you. You were an embarrassment to your wife, Monica. And whether you want to admit it or not, you are the one who was behind her death. If you had just kept your dick in your pants, she would still be alive today."

"You don't know what the hell you are talking about," William growled, moving so close that Rainier could smell the dank odor of his sweat and the stale scent of his hair oil. "We both know you're the murderer here. You killed my father. How else could you have known where to find his body? And it's a little odd, don't you think, that on your first day out of prison you would come home and dig him up? I think you just wanted to get him out of here before anyone else had a chance of finding his body. And then, when your family found out, they all came to bat for you." He pointed toward Wyatt. "Even your fucking brother."

"That's the dumbest thing I ever heard, William." Rainier balled his fists in an attempt to control his rage. All he wanted to do was reach up and tear out the man's throat. "For knowing so much about your father's remains, I would think you would know that, according to the medical examiner, he has been dead for around twenty-five years. That means I was just a toddler when your father died. I couldn't possibly have been the one to pull the trigger."

William glanced over at Wyatt as if gauging his reaction, to see whether or not Rainier was telling the truth.

"Don't look at my brother. You look at me."

William did so, then took a step back.

"I…I didn't know it happened that long ago. But that's no matter," William said, waving off Rainier's point. "You probably planted his body and made it look like it'd been there for a long time. It's probably just another one of your stupid games."

The man was grasping at straws and everyone knew it.

"William, ever since you started poking around I've been hearing about you and what you're capable of. Thinking back, if I had to bet, you are the one who is responsible for us finding your father's remains here."

"That's asinine. I have never wanted to hurt my own father. Unlike you."

The dam inside Rainier broke. Before he knew what he was doing, he reached up and took William by the throat. His fingers dug into the soft flesh around his trachea and squeezed. The little tube in his hand would have been so easy to crush. One motion and his family's nightmare would be over. Everything could go back to the way it had been before hell, in the form of William Poe, had rained down on them.

"No, Rainier. Don't do it," Laura begged. "He's not worth it. If you hurt him, your life is over."

He squeezed the man's throat just a little tighter. He was already violating his parol: if Rainier sacrificed himself by killing the man, at least he could say he had done something for his family—for the greater good.

"He isn't your father," Laura said. "If you kill him, it won't fix anything."

"But he's so goddamned evil. He has to be stopped," Rainier retorted, not looking away from William's eyes as they started to bug out of his head, thanks to the pressure he was creating by closing off the flow of air and blood.

"Let the judicial system take care of it, Rainier. We don't live in the Wild West anymore. Justice will come, but it's going to take time. We can't resort to violence or we're no better than animals, and you'd be no better than your father. Don't be like him, Rainier. If you love me at all, please…no…" she pleaded.

He let go of the man's neck, but there were impressions from where his fingers had gripped him. William slumped down to the ground, gasping and wheezing for breath. "Screw you," he whispered, his voice hoarse. "You're going back to prison if it's the last thing I do. Everyone in your family is going to pay for the mistake you just made," he said as he stood back up after regaining his breath.

Rainier looked at Laura. She had an expression of terror on her face, as if she knew that what William was saying was true. He had just violated his parole by assaulting the man.

If he was going to go back to prison, at least he would go for something he truly deserved to be punished for.

He leaned back and, with every bit of strength he possessed, struck. His fist connected with William's face. The scoundrel went flying across the snowy parking lot.

"Rainier! No!" Laura screamed.

Wyatt came running. "Goddamn it, Rainier!"

William lay on the ground, his back to them as he clutched his face. Blood speckled the snow, and Rainier watched a droplet melt the white crystals around it. He shouldn't have hit him, but he couldn't deny that it felt good to rain just a little bit of justice on the man who had wrought so much terror and tragedy on his family over the last few months. William deserved a hell of a lot more than just being punched in the face.

Leaving the man whimpering behind him, Rainier turned to face his brother and held up his hands. "Cuff me."

Wyatt reached down to his utility belt and grabbed his handcuffs. "I don't want to do this, Rainier. Why couldn't you just fucking control yourself?"

"That was control." Rainier looked down at his hands. Blood was dripping from his fingers, from where he had gripped his hands so tightly that his nails had cut through his skin.

Laura rushed to his side and threw her arms around him. "No. No. No," she repeated over and over, as if she just couldn't believe what had happened.

He wrapped his arms around her and smoothed her hair as he looked at her. "I made this choice. Good or bad, I have to pay the price. But know that I did this for my family, to make things right. It may seem stupid to you, and you have every right to be angry with me, but William had that coming."

"You wouldn't have done that if you loved me," Laura said.

His heart shattered under the pressure and weight of her words. "This doesn't have to do with the way I feel about you, Laura."

"Once again, Rainier, you're wrong." She let go of him and walked away toward the house. On her back was the blood from his hands.

Chapter Sixteen

After all they had talked about, and despite the consequences he must have known would follow, Rainier had still acted like he hadn't learned a thing in prison. He had failed and so had Laura. She couldn't save anyone—even those she had thought savable. He would never change. Her father had been right. Maybe she would have been better off just walking away.

She stood at the living room window and watched as Wyatt slipped the cuffs back onto his belt, unwilling to put them on his brother. Instead, he simply walked Rainier to his squad car and opened the back door, waiting for him to get in of his own accord. Watching him climb in was one of the hardest things she had ever witnessed. It was almost as if a piece of her was being sent back to prison with him—and in a way it was.

It had been a mistake to give him any of her heart.

Eloise walked up behind her and put her arm around her shoulders. "I'm so sorry, Laura."

Laura nodded.

"Are you going to go to the station with them?" Eloise asked.

"I…I can't. I can't watch him go back to that place."

She stared out at the back of Rainier's head as he sat in the car. William and Wyatt were talking, and William had a piece of gauze stuffed up his nose. He was speaking animatedly, his hands flying as he made angry gestures. She was sure he was telling Wyatt how he was going to continue tearing away at the family.

He may have deserved what he got, but no matter how much she empathized with Rainier's anger, she couldn't understand Rainier's choice. And maybe that, more than anything else, was the reason they truly couldn't be together. She couldn't be with a man who didn't harbor some level of self-control. There were always moments and situations in life when it would be easier to throw a punch and resort to violence, but that didn't mean people could allow themselves to act that way.

More than anything, he frightened her. This wasn't like the man she had come to know over the last few days. The one she had just seen seemed far too much like the other convicts she had known over the years. All the memories of convicts who had missed meetings, threatened her, showed up drunk or high—they all came to her at once. It may have been a stereotype of the ex-con, but it was a stereotype for a reason—those things were grounded in truth.

She had been stupid and naive to think Rainier was different.

Laura turned away from the window and embraced Eloise. She buried her face in the woman's neck and just let her tears fall. She didn't care that she barely knew her, or that she was making a show of herself. All she cared about was the ripping sensation in her chest as her heart was torn to pieces.

"I don't know what to say that will make you feel better, Laura," Eloise whispered. "Know that I'm hurting, too. I never wanted to see any of my sons being taken from me—and definitely not again."

She hadn't thought about how Rainier's mother must be feeling. It would of course destroy her from the inside out, as well. The poor woman had thought she would finally have her family all back together, and yet her dream was never realized. And though Eloise didn't know it yet, William had promised that their appeal for a payment plan would fail, which meant they'd be losing the ranch.

No matter how badly Laura's heart ached, Eloise was going through something so much worse—

losing her son, her family and the chances of keeping her beloved home, all in the same day.

The tears came more rapidly. As she hugged Eloise, Laura noticed faint shaking as the woman sobbed in her arms.

Whitney and Gwen were standing by the Christmas tree, their faces pale.

She wasn't going through this alone; she was going through it with the whole Fitzgerald clan. It was strange, but even though she had been around them for only a few days, she felt more like a part of this family than she ever had her own. They were all about love, support and understanding, not about who could get what from whom or how each of them could get ahead. It was just about the family and how they could be there for each other even when they didn't know what to say or do.

And yet her time with them was over; Rainier was gone. Any hope she'd had of saving him had disappeared with one perfectly placed punch, and the future that she had allowed herself to fantasize about for the last few days was just as unattainable as ever.

All she had was a houseful of Christmas decorations to go back to.

She pulled herself from Eloise's arms, trying to collect herself, just in time to see Wyatt and Rainier rolling out of the driveway. William Poe was already gone. It was over. Everything.

The smoke alarm started to beep and she glanced over at the kitchen, where smoke was billowing from the doorway toward the ceiling of the living room.

"Son of a—" Eloise said, charging toward the kitchen. "I must have left the bacon going."

"How much bacon did she cook?" Laura asked the two women by the tree, trying her hardest to focus on anything other than the tight pain in her chest.

"Oh, Eloise always does everything big. Everything," Whitney said with a smile as forced as Laura's words.

"I think she was really hoping that Waylon and Christina would come rolling in with Winnie this morning. And instead…" Gwen trailed off as she glanced out the window. "Do you think there's anything you can do, Laura?" she added.

Laura wanted to say yes, that she had the power to stop the train of destruction that was Rainier Fitzgerald, but she couldn't bring herself to lie to the woman. "I don't know," she said quietly.

Merle came into the house, and as he opened the door a cold, bitter breeze filled the living room, stealing all the fire's warmth.

"What are we going to do?" Whitney asked.

Laura was thankful she had spoken first, as she was afraid that if she had to ask about what had transpired she would dissolve into tears once again. She could fake strength for only so long before it would melt away and reveal the sensitive mess she was inside.

Merle closed the door and took off his coat.

She wasn't sure if he wasn't answering because he was afraid to tell them, or because he didn't want to tell *her*.

"You can tell us what happened, Merle. I'm sure I'll get a chance to read through Wyatt's report regardless of what transpires," Laura said, her voice cracking as she spoke. She coughed lightly, trying to clear the emotions from her throat.

He nodded. "William is obviously upset. He threatened to press charges, and well…we all know what will happen if he does." He laid his coat over his arm and stared at her as if there was something he wanted to say, but wasn't sure exactly how to say it.

He looked to the kitchen, where they heard the thump of a pan and the sound of running water. Thankfully, the smoke had stopped pouring through the doorway.

"Did you tell Eloise what William said…about the taxes?" Merle asked.

Maybe Laura had been wrong about the family. Maybe they weren't as supportive and forgiving as she had assumed.

"Really? Your son gets carted away to be processed, and yet here you are, worried about your taxes?"

"No, Laura, that's not it. I just…" He stared at the

kitchen door. "I just don't want to burden her with one more thing."

That she could understand.

"Sorry," she said, dabbing at a wayward tear that had escaped her. "I...I don't know what came over me..."

"You're fine. It's just a hard time. Trust me when I say that we are familiar with the strain," Merle said, sending her a soft, forgiving smile.

Gwen came over and took her hand. "No matter what happens, know that we're here for you."

Another unchecked tear slipped down Laura's cheek.

She had to stop crying. She couldn't be a mess like this over a man she had known for less than a week. She was a grown woman.

"Thank you," she said. "Really."

Gwen squeezed her fingers. "I know how much you love him. And I know what it's like to fall in love with one of the Fitzgerald men. They're wild and fiery—all of them. What Rainier did out there... it could have been any of those boys. They all love hard, and they defend even harder."

Laura wasn't sure how Gwen could say that any of the four sons could have assaulted William Poe. Wyatt wouldn't have. He had seemed to show incredible restraint when they had been outside, but then again maybe Gwen just knew him better.

She smiled in appreciation of Gwen's attempt to comfort her.

"I notice you're not denying the fact that you love him," Merle said. "I like that about you."

She opened her mouth to argue, to tell them all that they had her feelings toward Rainier all wrong. A few hours ago, she could have told them what she was feeling toward him was love, but now…she wasn't so sure.

Her phone rang. Pulling it from her pocket, she looked down at the caller ID. It was her father. Her chest constricted impossibly tighter, stealing her breath. He couldn't have already heard what had happened. Or maybe he could have.

William had probably called him from Dunrovin's driveway.

She hit Ignore.

It rang again. Couldn't her father get the hint that she didn't want to talk to him right now? The last thing she needed was further castigation.

She hit Ignore again.

And once more it rang.

"What?" she asked, finally answering the phone, as she knew full well that if she didn't he'd just keep on calling.

"I knew you were there," her dad said, his voice as gruff as her own. "I don't know why you think you can just stop answering me. It's convenient how you're happy to talk to me when you need something, but when I want to talk to you you're too busy."

That wasn't it at all, and he had to know that. He was just being an ass.

"The last thing I need right now is to get into a fight with you. What do you want?"

"I want you to check your attitude," he said.

No matter how old she got, she was sure that he would always treat her like she was some sixteen-year-old with an attitude problem. It only infuriated her more.

"If you're just calling to pick a fight, I need to go. I have better things to do."

"Those *better things to do* are why I'm calling. William Poe contacted me a few minutes ago. He was seeking representation."

Her stomach dropped.

"Do you know anything about Rainier Fitzgerald hitting him in the face? He said you would be available to act as a witness in his case."

She couldn't believe how quickly William was at it. She had been right; he'd probably called her father as soon as he'd gotten in his car.

"Are you going to take his case?"

There was a long silence on the other end of line. "I need to know a few things from you first, before I decide on anything. I need to be well informed. Is Rainier the man William makes him out to be?"

"I'm assuming you mean that William tried to tell you Rainier is a typical ex-convict."

She wanted to go to bat for Rainier and tell her father that he was different, but she couldn't bring herself to utter the words, as right now she wasn't so sure.

"It would be foolish of me," her father continued, "to think he was anything otherwise. Based on the way I saw you looking at him the other day, I'm a little unsure of how to proceed with this."

So her father had noticed her attraction to Rainier, after all. She really needed to learn how to mask her emotions better.

"You know I'm not stupid, right?" she asked, in an attempt to maneuver around her father's question.

He wasn't really calling her about what he should do with William. No, he was calling to see where things stood between her and Rainier.

"What do you mean?" her father asked, an innocent inflection to his voice.

"You have taken on the Fitzgeralds as your clients. In such a case, it would be a conflict of interest if you were to take William on as a client, as well. So let's not beat around the bush."

Her father laughed. "Sometimes I forget how smart you are."

She wasn't sure how to take his backhanded compliment, so she ignored it.

"Why did you really call? Did you just want me to know that you knew about the events at Dunrovin?"

His laughter came to an abrupt stop. "That and to let you know that William Poe is gunning for them even more than he already was. I'm going to work at him from my side to see if I can get him to drop the charges against Rainier, but I don't know what I can do for sure. He seemed pretty upset when I talk to him on the phone a few minutes ago."

She was surprised by her father's willingness to lend a hand.

"What did William do to you, Dad? Why are you suddenly willing to fight him? And don't try to tell me that this has anything to do with justice or some altruistic need to help the Fitzgerald family."

Her father sucked in a long breath and exhaled into the phone. "Whether or not you believe me, I love you. Though I don't always agree with your choices, or the men you seem to be attracted to, that doesn't mean I'm going to let you find your way into trouble."

No matter what her father did, she would always have a habit of getting into trouble. But she appreciated the fact that her dad was stepping up and doing something for her for once, without some ulterior motive. At least she thought he didn't want anything from her, but she couldn't be sure. Only time would tell.

"You didn't answer my question about William. Did he do something to you, Dad? Something that you need retaliation for?"

"I don't know what kind of man you think I am, Laura, but you're wrong."

"After so many years of you showing me exactly what kind of many you are, I find it pretty hard to believe that you're doing this out of the kindness of your heart and because you love me. I'm sure you loved me a few days ago, when I first came to you about the Fitzgeralds' case, and then you weren't willing to take it on. I just want to know what made you change your mind."

"Let's just say that a few things came to light that I didn't know about before, a few things that have changed the way I feel about this community and the people within it. And let's leave it at that. But do know," her father added, "it truly is my love for you that is guiding me with all of this. And I have a feeling that it is your love that is guiding you."

Chapter Seventeen

He'd screwed everything up. His life. His freedom. His one chance at love. In a blink of an eye, he'd reverted back to the man he'd promised himself he'd never become again. He hated himself more than ever. And even more than that, he hated what he had done to Laura and the position he'd put her in. She'd vouched for him, she had gone to bat for him and she'd gotten her father to take on his family's case even when that meant putting herself in the path of her dad's wrath.

She done so much for him, and Rainier had repaid her by finding himself here, in the back of Wyatt's squad car.

He ran his hands over his face and let out a long sigh.

"I wish I could say I was surprised," Wyatt said, pouring salt in his wounds.

"You can just stop, Wyatt. Whatever you think

you need to say to me, just don't. If it helps, know that I am already beating myself up for the decision I made."

Wyatt looked at him in the rearview mirror. "You know, brother, if you hadn't done something, I don't honestly know how much longer I could've gone on listening to him."

Rainier was taken aback by his brother's admission. They hardly ever agreed on anything, especially not since he'd come home. It was an odd sensation to know that his brother felt in any way similar to him.

"So you're saying that you would've hit him in the face, as well?" he asked, a wicked grin on his lips.

Wyatt shrugged. "You know, in my line of work, hardly a day goes by without somebody mouthing off at me or telling me how I'm doing my job wrong. It takes a certain amount of willpower to not go off on every idiot who thinks he should open his mouth and say something stupid to me. Ninety-nine percent of the time I don't have a problem walking away and letting whatever they're saying roll off my back, but it's different when they're talking about my family and when they start dragging people I love through the mud."

He could only imagine the number of times over the years people had probably commented to Wyatt about what he, Rainier, had done, and how he'd ended up in jail.

"If that's true, I'm sure that you wanted to take a swing at someone many a time, thanks to me."

Wyatt chuckled as he turned the car down the main road that led into Mystery. "Right after everything with your birth father, things were a little rough. But once word got out about everything that led up to it, most of the community understood why you acted as you did. It probably didn't hurt that most people know and love our parents."

"I heard about Yule Night festival, and how the community came together to raise funds for the ranch. I can only imagine how hard it must be for Mom and Dad to be going through all this crap right now." He paused as he thought about how it had felt when his fist had connected with William. "I can't believe I made things worse."

"We'll see how this all plays out," Wyatt said. "Maybe if William is concentrating on taking you down, he won't be able to focus as much of his energy on going after the ranch."

Rainier tried to laugh, but the sound came out dry and forced. They sat in silence, letting the failed laughter die in the air between them.

It started to snow, and as the tiny flakes fluttered down from the sky, they caught the light and looked like glitter filling the air.

"What would happen if William didn't press

charges?" Rainier asked, hating to get his hopes up. "You know, not that he won't, but just in case?"

"Didn't like my plan, huh?" Wyatt asked, tapping his fingers on the steering wheel. "Let's face it, we both know that William isn't going to let what you did slide. He's going to do everything in his power to make sure you are sent back to prison."

"What if there weren't any witnesses to testify on his behalf?"

"What, are you thinking of taking us all out?" Wyatt teased. "If they put us under oath, we'll have to tell the truth. You know how it is, perjury and all."

"I know. I guess I'm just grasping at straws. I wouldn't want to put any of you at risk like that, anyway," he said, blowing out a long breath.

There was no getting out of this. What was done was done. Once again, he would just have to face the consequences for his actions.

"I'm glad to hear it," Wyatt said, checking his rearview mirror again.

Rainier turned to see what he was looking at. William was behind them in his sedan.

"Do you think he's going to follow us all the way to the station?"

Wyatt glanced up again. "Technically speaking, he has yet to file charges against you. I told him that in order to do so, he would have to come down to the station and sign some papers."

"I'm sure he won't miss the opportunity." Rainier had an insatiable urge to turn and give the man the bird, but this time he resisted. "Wait…if he hasn't signed anything, then am I really under arrest or are you just taking me in?"

"I didn't read you your Miranda rights, did I?"

A tremor of excitement moved through him. Maybe he wasn't as screwed as he had assumed. Maybe there was a way around this, after all; the chances weren't in his favor, but at least he could still hope.

As they neared town and the police department, Rainier wanted to turn around to watch what William did. He felt stupid for hoping that along the way the man would just turn off, go home and forget about what happened. Such ideas and desires were ridiculous. Even without looking behind him, he knew William would still be there. In fact, with everything involving Dunrovin over the last month, it seemed he was always there. Rainier had a feeling that, no matter what happened in the future, William Poe wouldn't be happy until he ruined their family and the ranch—even if that meant they all ended up dead. The thought made chills run down Rainier's spine.

"Did you look in William's car when he came to the ranch?" Rainier asked.

Wyatt shook his head. "Why?"

"Doesn't it strike you as just a little bit odd that he

would come out there, all by himself, and start harassing us? He had to have known that he wouldn't be welcome—that there was a hell of a good chance he wouldn't get out of there without getting his ass beat."

"He was provoking you. We already established this. So what does that have to do with his car? I'm not following."

"What if he was coming there to attack us?"

Wyatt sat in silence for a moment. "William Poe's many things, but stupid isn't one of them. And if he came after the family on our ranch with the intention of hurting us, that would be more than stupid. There's no way he would've walked away from something like that alive."

"Maybe that's why he lost his nerve," Rainier said. "Maybe once he saw us and got a chance to speak his piece, maybe he realized the error he was making."

Rainier couldn't stand it anymore. He turned around in his seat and stared out the back window. William was talking on the phone, and as he spoke his free hand flew in angry gestures. From the look on his face, he was yelling at someone.

They drew up at a stoplight. William and Rainier locked eyes, and the man stopped talking. Neither would look away, and even from that distance Rainier could see the distaste and hatred William held for him.

Wyatt started to drive forward as the light turned green, but instead of following them, William swung left.

"What the hell is he doing?" Rainier asked.

Wyatt peered out the window and watched as William's car disappeared down the road. "Who knows what that guy is up to."

They were only a block from the police department. If he was turning away, did that mean he wasn't planning on pressing charges? Or was he playing some kind of stupid mind game? Rainier wouldn't put it past him. He was certain he hadn't scared him away with simply a look. William wasn't that weak.

Wyatt parked the car in front of the station and opened the door for Rainier to get out.

As he stepped from the car, he took in a long breath of the cold winter air. For all he knew, it was his last breath of real freedom.

"What do you want to do?" Rainier asked.

"If he does show up and sign the documents, then it will be to your benefit if you stay here and prove to the courts that you didn't try to run, and you were trying to make the best of a bad situation. Maybe the judge will be more lenient and won't add more time to your sentence in prison."

He still had five years left on his sentence if he went back. Until now, he hadn't really thought about the fact that if William did press charges those five years could easily turn into ten. The realization made him nauseous. That would mean by the time he got out he very well could be thirty-six years old. He would have spent a third of his life behind bars. It would be such a waste.

"Then I guess we need to go inside," he said, but the words passed from him in the same way a judge would've passed a ruling—without emotion.

"Are you sure?" Wyatt asked. "If you wanted, the Widow Maker Ranch—you know, Gwen's family's spread—is buttoned up. They're about to put it on the market, and no one is living there. If you wanted to hide out for a little bit and let everything die down and see what happens, you could stay there and nobody would know where you were."

"You would know," he said, giving his brother a weak smile. "It would compromise your integrity if you had to lie for me. You can't get wrapped up in this. I can't let you put your career in jeopardy for me."

He appreciated what Wyatt was doing for him, and the offer he was making, but from the look on his face, his brother knew that it was unfeasible, as well.

"We'll get through this," Rainier said. "You just lead the way to where I need to wait for William. From there, I'll navigate this journey the rest of the way."

"No matter what goes down in there, I got your

back. No matter what's happened in the past, you're my brother. I'll always be your brother," Wyatt said.

Rainier wasn't a hugger, but right now it was the only thing he could think to do that could express the way he was feeling toward his older brother.

"Wyatt, I don't know what I'd do without you, man," he said, his voice cracking. "And hey, for what it's worth, I'm sorry."

Wyatt shrugged as Rainier stepped back and they let go of one another. "Like I said, if you hadn't gone after William, I'm not sure that I wouldn't have. Maybe, if nothing else, you saved me."

This relationship would be one of the things he would miss the most.

"If they lock me up, I want you to look after Laura."

Wyatt nodded. "She'll always be welcome at my home, and I know Mom loves her almost as much as you do." He walked toward the front doors of the station and, opening it, waited for Rainier to walk in ahead of him.

"Mom *has* taken a shine to her," Rainier said with a laugh. "Can you believe she asked her to spend Christmas with us the first time she met her?"

"You know Mom. She knows from the get-go whether or not she likes someone. If I were you, I'd take that as Mother's official seal of approval."

"What do you think of Laura?"

They walked into the main office, and the secretary behind the glass smiled at Wyatt and gave them a little wave as they made their way past her.

"I mean, aside from the fact that we shouldn't be together, that is," Rainier said.

"I know I told you that I didn't want to get wrapped up in all of your drama, but we both know it's too late to stop whatever is going on between you two. And believe me when I say I know better than anyone how the heart wants what the heart wants. I mean, just look at Gwen and me."

"How did you guys end up back together?"

"It's a long story, but after her sister was killed… we both realized that we were just *meant* for each other."

"What about her mother? Didn't she have something to say about it? Especially after Gwen's father was killed on the ranch after his accident with the hay tedder?"

"Oh, her mother had plenty of issues with our getting together." Wyatt paused. "Come to think of it, our story ain't that different from yours—a lot of people didn't want to see us end up together. But if it made one thing abundantly clear, it's that we don't get to pick who we fall in love with. And when it comes to true love, nothing and no one should get in the way."

They turned a corner in the hall that led to Wyatt's

office. Standing on the other side of his brother's office door was Mr. Blade, who was holding his briefcase.

Rainier came to a dead stop. "Shit. What is he doing here?"

"I was about to ask you the same thing. You think Laura called him or something?"

From where they were standing, Rainier couldn't see the lawyer's expression, but he wished he could so he'd have some clue as to what kind of hornet's nest he was walking into.

"You want to wait here?" Wyatt asked.

Rainier shook his head and then bulled his way into his brother's office. Mr. Blade looked a little shocked at his sudden appearance.

"Are you here to yell at me? Go right ahead. But know that whatever you have to say to me, it's not going to change my feelings about your daughter."

He shook his head. "No, my daughter is the reason I'm here right now," Mr. Blade said, raising a finger as if threatening. "Know that if you break her heart or if you continue to hurt her, I'll be far more dangerous to you than William Poe."

"I have no intention of hurting your daughter any more than I already have," Rainier said. But as he spoke to the man, he found that he couldn't look him in the eye, and instead focused on a forensics manual on his brother's bookcase behind him.

"I'm glad to hear it, but regardless of your intentions, it doesn't guarantee her safety."

Wyatt stepped forward. "No, but I do. If Rainier has to go back to prison, she won't be left out to dry."

Mr. Blade looked Wyatt up and down, weighing and measuring him in a glance, then cracked a smile. It was almost imperceptible, but Rainier had a feeling that was about as big as the lawyer's smile ever got.

"Laura wasn't wrong about you Fitzgeralds. You're good people." Mr. Blade sat down in front of Wyatt's desk. "And that's why I'm here today. I already heard what happened with William."

"Did Laura call you?" Rainier asked, a bit surprised that she would've already reached out to her father.

"No, William did."

Apparently, being good people wasn't enough to keep them on good terms with her father.

"Sir, are you here to let us know that you've decided not to take our family's case?" Rainier inquired.

"Far from it." The little smile on Mr. Blade's face disappeared. "In fact, he asked my firm to help him file assault charges against you. However, due to recent findings, I had to decline. I may have mentioned to him that if he wished to pursue assault charges against you, it would force my hand in acting upon your family's case, and we would be moving to court more rapidly than I intended."

"What did you find? And does that mean he's not pressing charges?" Rainier asked, a sense of excitement moving through him.

Mr. Blade nodded. "I think he realized it would be in his best interest to simply put what happened between you two at the ranch behind him. However, I strongly recommend that you do not act on your impulses again. If you were dealing with any other parole officer besides my daughter, I am sure that by now you would have already found yourself behind bars. You're just lucky that she likes you, and you have a brother who is in law enforcement. Professional favors can go a long way, but they can't keep you safe forever."

Rainier was glad he was sitting down, as he feared his knees would have given out on him had he been standing. "Thank you so much, Mr. Blade. I can't tell you how much that means to me. How relieved I am. I'm so sorry that all this happened. I swear I won't let it happen again."

"See to it that it doesn't." Mr. Blade reached down to his briefcase. He pulled out a series of papers and laid them on Wyatt's desk. "Now, to the other business at hand and what we managed to find… Have you ever talked to your parents about how they came into possession of the Dunrovin Ranch?"

The brothers looked at one another questioningly, and Wyatt shook his head.

"I had a feeling that may have been the case." Mr. Blade tapped the paper on top of the stack. "We managed to find the bill of sale on the property. Did you know that Dunrovin Ranch was on the chopping block twenty-five years ago?"

"What do you mean, on the chopping block?" Rainier asked, peering at the stack of papers. The page on top looked like a jumble of legalese that only a lawyer could understand.

"I mean it was up for auction. From what I could find out from the paperwork, the family who owned the ranch before lost it in a situation very similar to that of your parents."

"That's impossible. William Poe has been a tax appraiser only for the last ten years. He couldn't have screwed anyone over twenty-five years ago," Wyatt said, taking his seat behind the desk.

"You're right," Mr. Blade said with a nod. "He wasn't screwing anyone out of their land twenty-five years ago. No, it was actually his family who had owned it before you and yours."

"No!" Wyatt dropped his hands down on the desk with a thump. "That can't be true. Mom and Dad said they had gotten it from a family who had decided they didn't want to be ranchers anymore."

Mr. Blade's eyebrows rose in surprise. "I think

your parents may have been lying to you. From the looks of it, William's father, Paul, had lost the property due to a tax lien. When the place went to auction, the Poes had thought they would be able to buy it back. However, your parents came in and bought it out from under them."

"Does he think he can recreate the same chain of events? Is this some twisted attempt to pay my parents back for getting the ranch?" Rainier asked.

"I have no idea what William Poe is thinking," Mr. Blade said. "But if I can prove that he is behind these taxes and is doing it so he can buy the ranch, I think we have a really strong case, as we certainly have found a motive for his erratic behavior."

"Thank you, Mr. Blade," Rainier said. "We'll see if—"

"Wait." Wyatt interrupted with a wave of his hand. "What about the body? How did Paul Poe's remains end up on the ranch?"

"That's one thing I can't make heads or tails of," Mr. Blade said. "But we are going to have to hope that your parents had nothing to do with his death. If they did, everything we're working toward is going to go up in smoke."

Chapter Eighteen

He couldn't believe his parents had lied to him. Surely their lie had been well intended, and they had never thought it would come back to haunt the family, and yet here they were. Or maybe Merle and Eloise had been kept in the dark about the circumstances in which the ranch had gone up for auction. Since they had bought it before the days when a person could Google just about anything, perhaps they hadn't been told who the ranch had once belonged to. Rainier had to hope that his parents weren't involved in anything that would cast a bad light upon the family.

Wyatt turned the squad car down the road to the ranch, and as they drew nearer to home, Rainier's stomach tightened. He was more nervous now to face his mother and father than when he'd been released from jail. It was one thing for him to know he was guilty of wrongdoing, and another to think that his family may have been guilty, as well.

"Do you realize today's Christmas Eve?" Wyatt asked, looking over at him in the passenger seat.

"Damn." He had barely thought of anything beyond what they were dealing with and what was happening between him and Laura. Somehow the date had slipped through the cracks. He had no presents for anyone. Hopefully, the family wouldn't be even more disappointed with him than they already were. He was so tired of feeling like a disgrace. With every choice he made it seemed he was screwing up.

If this was what life on the outside was, he wasn't sure which lifestyle—his present situation or prison—was harder. At least in jail very little was expected of him. Yet he could never let himself go back to that place. It killed his soul. "I'm sure you haven't gotten the chance to pick anything up for Laura, but in my experience women tend to like what comes from the heart the most."

"So you think I should write her a love poem? 'Roses are red, violets are blue...'" he said with a laugh.

"That's not what I meant, smart-ass. But I'm glad you're feeling good enough to be your normal smart-mouthed self."

"It's amazing what not going back to prison can do for a man," Rainier said with a smile.

"Do you know if your birth father is still alive?" Wyatt asked.

Why was he bringing that up right now?

"Did you hear something?"

Wyatt shook his head. "No. I'm just thinking about what happened with you and him. If you saw him again, do you think you would do to him what you just did to William Poe, or would you do something worse?"

"You know how I feel about what happened with William. I won't make the same mistake. And with my father, if he's still alive and if I see him, I think I would turn around and walk away. One thing I did learn in prison is that the worst punishment someone can undergo is isolation. The mind does strange things when you're forced to be alone with it, and think about all the mistakes you've made. All I can hope is that my father, like William Poe, is haunted by his wrongdoings."

"You should make that into a Hallmark card, man," his brother said, giving him a soft punch to his upper arm, reminding him exactly what it was and how it felt to be brothers.

Wyatt parked the car next to Laura's and chuckled as he noticed the reindeer antlers on her doors. "Those are hilarious. Gwen would love something like that. She's all about Christmas stuff. Now that her mom's in rehab for her alcoholism, she grabbed all of their old decorations and brought them over to my place. It's like Santa's workshop in there."

"Laura's house is the same way. Heck, it might even be worse. Her house actually *is* Santa's workshop. She was telling me that she makes and sells Christmas decorations online."

"You mean like on Etsy or something?"

He had no idea what Etsy was, but he nodded. "She seems to really enjoy it."

At the thought of Laura, all that they had last said to one another and what had happened between them, Rainier stopped in his tracks and stared up at the front door. He glanced over at her car, surprised that she was still here and hadn't gone home.

"It's going to be okay, man," Wyatt said.

"No. I have a feeling that I'm not gonna have time to worry about a Christmas gift or lack of one for Laura. She must hate me. And she has every right to. I can't believe what I did to her. How she must feel. I put her in an impossible situation."

"You made a mistake, Rainier, and thankfully, you avoided trouble by the skin of your teeth. I think she's just gonna be excited to see you. I can tell from the way you two look at each other that you guys are in love. And when you love each other, I mean really love each other, you can get through a lot."

"But when is it too much?"

"*Too much* isn't really something that applies

when you love. Because you can never really love someone too much. All that love equates to a lifetime of learning to forgive one another, and accepting the person for who they really are—stupid decisions, screwups, bad sense of humor and all."

"Hey, I'm not the one with the bad sense of humor," Rainier joked.

It all came down to this. If she loved him like Wyatt assumed, she would forgive him. And if she couldn't move past this, and it was *too much*, then what he was feeling toward her wasn't being reciprocated and he would have to take a few steps back. It would never work if they weren't in the same emotional place.

He and Wyatt made their way into the ranch house. His heart hammered away inside his chest as they walked into the living room. It was unusually quiet, so much so that the only sound he could hear was the erratic thump of his heartbeat.

"Hello?" Wyatt called.

No one answered.

"Maybe they're out in the main office. Did you notice if the lights were on or anything?" Rainier asked.

"It was dark out there."

"Weren't Waylon, Christina and Winnie coming back to the ranch today?" Rainier asked. "Maybe they called and everyone ran to the airport to pick them up."

"Everyone? Even Laura?" Wyatt said. "No, something's not right." He reached down and put his hand on his Glock.

Rainier chuckled, trying to make light of the situation even though he was just as nervous about his family's disappearance. "I don't think you really need to take things there, do you?"

Wyatt dropped his hand, but Rainier could see his fingers twitching as if he wanted to reach back up and take hold of his gun once again.

"Let's take a look around and see if we can find them. Did you at least text Mom or Gwen?"

Wyatt got his phone and quickly tapped away, then slipped it back in his pocket. "You're right. I'm sure this is all nothing and everyone is fine. What can I say? I'm just a little bit jumpy after everything that's been going on at the ranch lately." He gave a light laugh.

"While we wait for them to get back to us, let's go check around the barn. Or maybe they're in the pasture or something. I'm sure we'll run across them."

They made their way outside and over to the barn. The door was partly open and Rainier was met with a thin shaft of light. Relief swept through him as his mother's voice filled the air.

"We didn't mean for anything to happen with

your brother, your wife or your girlfriend. We never wanted anything bad to happen to you," Eloise was saying.

He looked inside the barn, but from where he was standing he couldn't see anyone. He started to walk inside, but Wyatt held him back and shook his head. His palm was back on his weapon.

"You're making a huge mistake," Laura said, her voice high and tense.

"You would know all about mistakes, wouldn't you, Ms. Blade? I can't believe you would be stupid enough to find your way into that lowlife Rainier's bed. You could've done so much better, and I know your father doesn't approve." William Poe's voice filtered down from the hayloft above.

"I don't care what you think about my life. As far as I can tell, you have no room to judge anyone else for their personal life," Laura said.

Rainier loved the defiance in her voice. She was so strong. Yet mouthing off to William was probably not the smartest thing she could have done. Then again, he had no right to judge another's approach to dealing with that man.

"Yes, I heard all about what your father intends to do. He is a fool if he thinks he can go against me. I always get what I want."

"Really?" Merle asked. "If that's the case, then why are you here? If you thought you really had a chance at having us give up on this ranch and letting it get taken by the state, then you wouldn't be standing here holding that gun."

Gun?

William had to be desperate. From everything Rainier had heard and everything his mother had told him, the man was conniving and smart, but he always sent other people to do his dirty work for him, whether it be Waylon's ex-wife, Alli, or someone else. He was always careful to keep himself out of the limelight. Which meant in this case, he didn't intend on letting anyone walk away to become a potential witness.

He and Wyatt had to get in there and help their family and Laura. They'd have to move fast. No doubt William was going to kill them and anyone else who stumbled onto the scene.

"You don't know what you're talking about, old man," William yelled. "I'm just tired of screwing around with you people. I'm tired of you all getting people I care about hurt or killed."

"We didn't have anything to do with your wife's murder or your brother's incarceration. You did all that, William," Merle said. "You don't get to point your finger at us because you had to deal with the consequences of your choices. You need to take accountability for your actions."

"I don't know who you think you are to tell me

how I should and shouldn't act," William said. "You're not my father."

Rainier looked over at Wyatt and his brother cringed. No one spoke to Merle like that and got away with it.

"Besides," William continued, "it's your fucking fault that my father wasn't around. You are all nothing but murderers."

"We had nothing to do with your father's death, William," Merle argued.

"Then how did he die on this ranch? I'm sure it wasn't just some coincidence that after you stole the property from underneath us, he went missing, and then twenty-five years later his remains are found here. Knowing this family, he probably came out here and you all shot him."

"Why would we shoot him?" Merle asked.

William snorted in anger. "He probably realized that you guys were never going to let him win at that auction—no matter how high he went. You must've known in advance what his max amount was. You probably paid somebody off, and then when it came down to business, your underhandedness got you this place. He probably came out here in search of revenge for what you did. And you managed to pull the trigger first."

There was a click and slide, like the sound of a round being jacked into the chamber of a gun.

"But you won't get the drop on me," William continued. "Not like you did with my father. I'm going to get this ranch. And I'm going to get my revenge. My sweet, sweet revenge."

There were the sounds of a scuffle.

"Don't you dare touch me," Laura said.

William gave a mocking laugh. It was too much for Rainier to take. They had to get in there. Rainier motioned for them to move forward. Wyatt nodded and stepped ahead of him, pulling his gun from his holster.

Damn, he wished he could have a gun. Standing there, watching his brother take the point position, ready to face whatever firestorm they were walking into, Rainier felt ridiculous and ill-prepared. He had no way to protect the people he loved. The only thing going for him and Wyatt was the fact that it didn't seem as though William knew they had returned. The element of surprise was on their side.

Wyatt eased into the barn, and taking a low ready position, flagged the main area. A couple horses had their heads over their gates, peering out at them. One, a black mare, greeted them with a soft nicker.

Rainier lifted his finger to his lips, instinctively motioning for the horse to be quiet. As he realized what he'd done, he felt ridiculous. Laura would've loved to see him do that. No doubt she would have laughed at him.

He glanced up to the hayloft. Laura's feet were sticking over the side, her high heels hanging off her feet. From the angle of her feet, she must have been lying on her stomach, as if she were a prisoner who had been told to hit the ground in an officer's attempt to neutralize a possible threat.

William had his back to Rainier as he stood at the edge of the hayloft. He leaned against one of the support beams. There was a gun in his right hand, but it hung limp at his side.

At least they weren't in immediate danger. Yet Rainier had no idea how Wyatt intended for them to get up to there and take down William before he noticed them. From the main floor of the barn they would lose any gunfight.

They would have to outsmart the man.

He tapped Wyatt's shoulder and motioned for his brother to follow him outside. They retreated slowly, easing out of the door.

"You need to call backup," he whispered. "There's no way we can get the drop on him."

Wyatt took out his phone and tapped another message. "Done, but it's gonna take some time for anyone else to get out here. Most everybody's home with their families because of the holiday."

Of course. Rainier hadn't thought of the fact that the department would be running on a skeleton crew.

Though it made sense, as they had seen very few other officers coming and going at the station.

As he thought about it, it struck him as a bit odd that Mr. Blade had been working. But maybe a man like him never really took a day off. Maybe he had more in common with his daughter than Rainier had originally assumed.

"In the meantime, we are going to have to figure this out ourselves," he whispered.

Before his brother had time to react, Rainier pushed Wyatt out of view from anyone inside the barn, and made his way back inside. The door screeched as metal ground on metal when he opened it wider.

"Hello? Anyone out here?"

There was the sound of footsteps on the wood floor above as William turned to face him, but the man kept his gun out of sight. "Rainier, just the man I wanted to see." There was a large cut along the arch of his cheekbone, right under his eye. It was puffy and his eye was so swollen that Rainier doubted he could see out of it. He chalked it up to advantage number two. Though maybe it was really number one, now that they no longer had the element of surprise.

"I see you're not gonna be winning any beauty contests in the near future, William," Rainier said with a dry laugh. "Then again, even without that shiner, I don't think you had much going for you in the looks department."

William produced the gun and aimed it at him. "Say hello, Laura. It may be the last chance you get to talk to your lover boy."

Laura gasped and he heard her as she rolled over and sat up at the edge of the loft. It looked as though her hands were tied behind her back, but besides her arms being immobilized, she appeared unharmed. "Rainier, what are you doing here?"

He smiled. "Turns out I had an unexpected ally who helped keep me from going back to jail. You know, your father isn't half-bad."

"Did he know you were coming back—"

"Shut up, woman," William said, shoving her away from the edge until she was out of view.

Wyatt wouldn't be able to take a shot at William. Not from here. Not with everyone out of view and so close to the man. One stray bullet and someone else could be killed. He couldn't risk their lives.

"Don't talk to her like that," Rainier said, forcing William's attention back to him and away from the woman he loved.

"You really are stupid, man," he retorted, pointing the gun at him.

"I'm not the stupid one, William. I'm not the one who just took four people hostage with the intention of murdering them."

"Are you really going to think you're better than me? You think you can judge what I'm doing? You are trash. Your opinion is of no matter to me."

"William," Eloise called out, an edge of panic in her voice. "I know what happened to your father."

What was his mother doing? William was angry, and who knew what he was capable of. In a split second, he could point the gun and pull the trigger, killing her.

"What in hell are you talking about?" William spat.

"You were right," she continued. "Your father came out here to get his revenge. He was hoping, just like you are now, that if he killed us maybe he would get another chance at buying back your family's ranch."

"So you killed him?" William asked.

"No, nothing like that." Eloise's voice was soft, almost apologetic. "In those days, do you remember your family's old barn? It was about a hundred feet or so from where we are now. Your father was standing in front of it when I came out and found him. He was smoking a cigarette. You know, everyone smoked back in those days, but even so there was an unwritten rule that no one smoked near a barn. You couldn't put the animals at risk. I told him to put it out. Instead, he threw it back behind him, straight into a haystack."

"My father would never put animals at risk. No matter what you say, he wasn't a monster. He just had a run of bad luck, then more, when you guys moved into Mystery."

"I'm telling you the truth, William," Eloise said. "Everything caught on fire. It was an inferno in no time. Unfortunately, I was there alone that night. Merle had gone into town to meet up with an old veteran friend of his. Before I could run inside and call the fire department, your father was on me."

"Shut your mouth right now, you lying bitch. My father would never have touched you," William seethed.

"He put the gun to my head, but I struggled. I don't know what happened, but somehow in the fight, the gun went off. I swear I didn't pull the trigger. Your father's death was just a horrible accident."

William leaned against the support beam. He lowered the gun slowly, but it was still pointed in the direction Rainier assumed his mother was sitting.

"You're wrong. It doesn't make any sense. There's no way…" William said, stunned. "If that's true, that it was nothing more than an accident, why didn't you report his death to the police?"

There was a long pause.

"You have to understand, William," Merle said, "it was around that time we were trying to adopt the boys. Adoption is a very tough process. If an agency caught wind of anything like that happening…we would've never gotten our sons. We would've never gotten the chance to help all those kids in need."

"My mother deserved to know. I deserved to know what happened to my father. Do you have any idea how many years I've been searching for him?" William asked.

"We're so very sorry," Eloise said. "We couldn't tell you. We couldn't risk everything. Our lie has haunted us for so long, and I'm sorry you had to find out like this. But you need to put your gun down. If you do, we can forgive you. No one has to know about this. You forgave Rainier and didn't press charges, and we will return the favor."

"Shut up," William said, running his free hand over his face. "I can't hear any more of your garbage."

"If it makes you feel better, William," Eloise said, "I was the one who buried your father. I made sure to say a few kind words and give him a little service out of respect for you and your family."

"You mean right after you killed him? If you did anything kind, it was out of guilt and not some self-less act." William pushed the gun into the waistband of his pants. "Get down there with your son." He pointed toward Rainier.

What was the man doing? Was he going to have

Eloise climb down from the loft so he could have an easier target?

His mother slowly made her way down the ladder. Turning, she saw Rainier and threw her arms around his neck. "I'm so glad you're here. I hope you know how much I love you."

From the way she spoke, it sounded as if she was afraid they would be her last words.

"Get down here, William," Rainier ordered. "You don't get to stand up there and pretend like you're some big shot. If you are going to kill us, do it like a real man. I want to look you in the eyes when you pull that trigger."

William's laughter filled the air and the shrill sound spooked several of the horses. They squealed as they panicked and paced around inside their stalls.

William climbed down the ladder, watching Rainier carefully as he stepped onto the ground. "Not as much of a chicken shit as I thought you were." He pulled the gun from his pants and pointed it between Rainier's eyes. "I'm going to kill Laura last. I want her to watch as your family is wiped off this planet."

In a flash of movement, Rainier reached up and took hold of the gun, stepping out of its sights. It went off. The bullet lodged into the ground at their feet. The boom echoed through the cavernous barn as the scent of gunpowder thickened the air. The shot was so loud it made his ears ring. Yet he could still hear the cry of the animals as they panicked.

He tried to twist the weapon, breaking William's grip. But the man was stronger than he looked, or perhaps just as driven by rage and fury as he was. Rainier elbowed William in the chest and twisted the gun again, this time breaking his hold. Grabbing the weapon, he stepped back and pointed it at William.

All he had to do was pull the trigger. This would all be over. His family would be safe.

If he pulled it, his actions would be justified. It would be in self-defense. But he'd made a promise to his brother, and he couldn't compromise Laura again. He'd already gotten lucky once today in escaping the vise-like grip of prison.

William smiled nervously. "Just put the gun down. I know you don't have what it takes to pull that trigger. I was wrong about you before. You may be an ex-con, but you're not a murderer."

For once, the man was right. Rainier had no desire to take a life, not even William's, when push came to shove. He'd never be able to look at himself in the mirror again, knowing what he'd done.

He took his mom by the arm and slowly moved back toward the door. Leaning close, he whispered, "Wyatt's outside. Wait for the police."

If he could hold off William for just a little bit longer, he and everyone else in his family could get out of this without having to make a terrible decision—whether or not to take a life.

He let go of Eloise, and she disappeared into the darkness. Wyatt was nowhere to be seen. Rainier threw the gun away. It thumped down into the grass of the yard, but he couldn't have said exactly where.

It was better this way.

William laughed. As Rainier turned to face him once again, he found the barrel of a revolver pointed directly at him.

"No man goes to battle with just one weapon." William cocked the gun.

A shot rang out through the air.

William crumpled to the ground. Blood poured from the hole in his head. It spread out in a macabre crimson pool and started to leach into the muck and used hay that littered the floor.

Standing at the barn's side door, a few feet from the body, was Wyatt.

His brother had pulled the trigger. He'd saved Rainier's life.

Wyatt was still aiming his gun at the body as if he was worried that the dead man would rise again. But William Poe wouldn't be coming back. He'd never again terrorize their family.

Chapter Nineteen

The next morning, the ranch was quiet and still after a night of frenetic activity. There had been news trucks and cars of inquisitive friends and neighbors filling the parking lot until the wee hours of the morning. Every time Rainier thought about last night, all he could envision was William's body lying in a pool of blood as reporters' cameras flashed wildly, casting eerie shadows throughout the barn.

Rainier held Laura in his arms as they stood at the living room window, looking outside, as he thought about everything that had happened. Even though they hadn't stepped out-of-doors since last night, Laura still felt cold to his touch.

She had been through so much that he wasn't sure what he could do to help her get through this in as healthy a way as possible. When they had gone to bed, it was more symbolic than anything else, as neither had slept. Instead, they had lain there holding one another. It was cathartic and comforting to have her in his arms, and to listen to the calming sound of her breathing.

There was no longer any question in his mind or in his heart—they were meant to be together. When he was with her, it was as if he inherently knew everything would be okay. No matter what life threw at them, they would make it, as long as they were together.

"Heck of a way to spend Christmas Day, isn't it?" Rainier said.

She smiled at him, but didn't say anything and stepped out of his arms. She walked over to the windows and pulled the cord that released the drapes, shutting out the world.

"I have thought about it a lot, and every time, I come back to one thing—William Poe got what he deserved," Laura said. "He was crooked. And he had a hand in each of the deaths that happened over the last month. He thought he was above the law, and that if he just threw enough money and power behind issues and pulled enough political strings, he would get away with whatever he wanted. His only goal in life was to hurt other people."

"You're right, Laura. But don't forget about yourself. What William did to you was inexcusable. And as long as I live, I'll never let anyone lay their hands on you like he did."

She smiled, and some of the stress and exhaustion that had blanketed her seemed to lift. "As long as you live? That sounds like some kind of promise." There was an edge of playfulness to her voice.

"It would be, if you allowed me the honor."

She opened her mouth to speak, but a sudden patter of footsteps sounded in the hall. Winnie, Waylon's two-year-old daughter, ran into the living room. Her brunette hair was plastered against the side of her face and there were sleep marks on her cheeks. She must've slept hard after she, Waylon and Christina arrived on a midnight flight.

"Did Santa come?" she asked, her words the rushed and garbled ones of a toddler.

Laura walked over and squatted down at her eye level. "Did you look over there?" Smiling, she pointed at the hearth, where the mantel was covered in Christmas stockings. "But I think before you open any of the presents you should go get your dad and Christina. And I bet Nana and Gramps wouldn't want to miss all the fun, either."

Winnie looked over Laura's shoulder and stared longingly at the large stack of presents under the stockings, decorated with Disney princesses and shiny bows. "Can I just open one?" the little girl asked, and gave Laura a pleading look.

"No, little miss." She stood up and put her hand on the little girl's back. "You run along and wake everyone up, and I'll go get some hot chocolate ready. How many marshmallows would you like? Wait, I bet you don't even like marshmallows, do you?"

Winnie looked up at her as if she had lost her mind. "I *love* mushmellows."

"Well, I better give you a couple extra," Laura said.

The toddler turned and ran down the hall, banging on doors and calling out the names of family members as she rushed to wake them.

Laura laughed. "I guess I'm going to need your help finding the ingredients for hot chocolate in your parents' kitchen. Would you mind?"

"Whatever you need. Like I said, I'll always be there." Rainier took her hand and they walked together into the kitchen.

Seeing her with Winnie made him love her that much more. Laura was incredible. And it was incredible how well she fit into his family. It was almost as if there had always been a place for her. As soon as she'd walked into their lives, she had taken on the role she had always been meant to have.

"Do you think Wyatt is going to be okay?" she asked as she walked over and took mug after mug from the cupboard.

"As far as I know. He's on paid leave, just as long as it takes to investigate everything that happened and clear him of any wrongdoing. It shouldn't take long, as he did what any officer would have done."

Laura nodded and walked over to the refrigerator and took out the milk. "I'm glad to hear it. I know you and Wyatt had your problems, but just like you and the rest of your brothers, he's a good man. In fact, you have a wonderful family."

One he hoped she would join someday. If he was going to ask her to marry him, he wanted to do it once and he wanted to do it the right way. She deserved the very best. She always would.

"I'm lucky." He took the milk from her hand and set it beside the stove as he stood in front of her. He wrapped his arms around her.

"Are you now?" she said, smiling up at him. "How so?"

"Are you fishing for compliments?" he teased, rubbing his thumb on the small of her back.

"Would that be so bad?" she asked.

"Not at all." He pressed a gentle kiss to her forehead. She smelled of his fresh sheets and faintly of cinnamon and cloves. "I've never been luckier than when I walked out those gates at the prison and saw you. You took my breath away. It was like some kind of dream—me finding my freedom and you, all in the same seconds. And ever since that moment, all I've wanted is to be close to you. You were my Christmas miracle, and I want to be with you for the rest of my life."

Her arms tightened around him as she giggled.

"You say that now, but are you going to be able to put up with all my quirks? I mean, you haven't seen me in craft mode. You know, felt flying everywhere, hot glue guns and sequins, the whole shebang."

He laughed as he imagined her with glue in her hair and a sequin stuck to her forehead. "I think that would only make you that much more lovable."

"Lovable?" she asked with a quirk of her brow.

"Well, I was going to say beautiful, but you are already the most beautiful woman I've ever seen. With or without sequins, you will always be stunning."

She smiled, and her whole face brightened. "Wow, you are quite the charmer this morning."

"Are you going to answer my question?" he asked, his hands becoming sweaty as he grew more nervous.

"What question?" she teased.

"You know darn well what question."

"If we do this I'm going to have to quit my job," she said, but she didn't look unhappy about the prospect. "Someone else would have to take on your case."

"If you want to quit, you could. I don't care about who has my case—I'm not going to cause any more trouble," Rainier said. "Think about it. You could focus on your business. I have always thought the best investment people can make is in themselves. You could follow your dreams. And I could go to work here at the ranch. They are starting to book up for next summer. I could be a handyman or something around here. So we have that figured out. Now, what do you say?"

She stepped back from him, her hands on his waist. "I don't see a man on his knees. I thought that was, like, a requirement. You know, if a guy was to make some kind of request that included something like marriage, or whatever."

From the way she spoke, he could tell she was just as nervous as he was.

"Gosh, you are so demanding. Are you always going to be like that?" He gave her a playful, inquisitive glance.

"Hey, take it or leave it, Mr. Charm. I'm always going to be the imperfect and wonderful me."

"And it is all of you that I love. I'd never want you to change." He slipped his hands into hers as he got down on one knee in front of her.

"You love me?" She smiled.

"More than anything in the entire world."

"Good, because I love you, too." She leaned down and kissed the back of his hand. "And if we're going to do this…if we're going to have a life together… I don't want to start it out on uneven footing. I want us to always be best friends, for us to walk side by side. I never want you to feel like you need to kneel to me."

"But you just told me—"

She laughed. "Welcome to my world. I guess I want what I want, but there's a part of me—the little girl who's always had a dream of this moment—who wants the tradition." She squeezed his hands. "How about this?" She got down on her knee, so they were face-to-face. "From this moment on, I want us to be equal partners."

Just when he thought he couldn't love her more, she did something like this.

"We can have any life you dream of, just as long as you promise to be my wife. I don't have a ring, but if I did it would have a green emerald at its center and I'd have it in a red velvet box—all Christmas for you. More, it would be a symbol of how rare our love is." He kissed her knuckles and pressed their entwined hands against his chest, where he was sure she could feel his heart thrashing wildly. "Laura Blade, will you marry me?"

The door to the kitchen flew open and Winnie came rushing in, not stopping until she stood so close to him they nearly touched. "They ready," she said, breathless and unaware of her intrusion. "Dad wants two mushmellows."

Laura laughed at the girl and her cute mispronunciation. "Coming right up, sweetheart."

She moved to stand up, but he stopped her. "Please, answer me." He didn't care if he sounded like he was begging. He couldn't go another moment without knowing her answer.

Laura looked him in the eyes. "Rainier Fitzgerald,

I would be honored to spend the rest of my days with you. You have brought me a happiness that I didn't know I could feel. I love you and I know that I will only grow to love you more and more each day that we spend together."

"You guys gettin' married?" Winnie said, but it was as much a proclamation as it was a question.

"Is that okay with you?" Rainier asked.

"Hmm…" She popped her thumb in her mouth and answered with a simple nod. Just as quickly as she had appeared, she turned around and ran to the door of the kitchen. "They gettin' married!"

There was the sound of cheers and clapping from the living room.

"I hope you didn't want to keep it a secret," Rainier said with an apologetic tilt of his head. "With this crew, it seems like most secrets tend to come out. It's only a matter of time."

"Even those about dead bodies," Laura murmured.

He laughed. "You make a good point, but I'm hoping that kind of a secret was a onetime thing."

"I certainly hope so, but you're not allowed to go digging around anymore spigots. Deal?"

He stood up and held out his hand to help her stand. "You got it, my love. No spigots."

They finished making the hot cocoa and carried trays of drinks out to the living room. All three of his brothers and their fiancées were sitting on the couches, and his mother and father were in their chairs. Everyone looked up at them as they came into the room. His mother jumped to her feet and, as soon as he set the tray on the living room table, threw her arms around him and then Laura.

"Congratulations, you two! I couldn't be happier," she said, tears running in wild rivers down her face. But she didn't seem to notice or care. "With Wyatt and Gwen's wedding, and now this…all our boys are getting married!"

His father gave them each a hug. "Anything you need, you two. Anything at all. We're here for you." He turned to face the others. "And that goes for all of you. You are always welcome in our home and in our lives. You are the reasons we do what we do. You are the reason we fight. And no matter what the future brings, we will always fight for this family."

As Merle spoke, Rainier thought of the threat that still loomed over them. There was still the matter of the taxes. Just because William Poe was dead didn't change the fact that they still needed to pay what they could and get legal proceedings together to fight the state in court. The battle was won, but the war was far from over.

He couldn't let what he couldn't control destroy or tarnish Christmas. They had tomorrow and the next day and the next to fight, but for now all they needed was each other, and all *he* needed was Laura. The rest of the world could wait.

Winnie took a long slurp of hot chocolate from her Minnie Mouse mug. The sound made everyone smile.

"Hey, Win, why don't you help me hand out the presents and stockings?" Waylon asked.

She thumped down her cup, sloshing chocolate on the table.

As they handed out gifts, no one opened theirs except Winnie, who tore through the wrapping and bows and squealed as she uncovered trucks, Legos and a collection of plastic horses. Eventually, Waylon went to the front door, motioning for Rainier to stay quiet as he slipped outside.

A few minutes later a knock sounded.

Rainier walked over and, expecting Waylon, opened the door. "Need help?" he asked. But he stopped when he saw Mr. Blade standing there, an envelope in his hand.

"I hope you don't mind. I knew my daughter was here for Christmas, so I knew you all were home. I didn't want to intrude, but I have a gift for your mother and father."

"Come on in," he said, motioning for him to step inside.

"Mr. Blade, we're so glad you stopped by," his

mom exclaimed, as if she had been expecting the man on Christmas Day.

"Thank you, Eloise." He walked over to her and handed her the envelope.

The front door opened again, and Waylon walked in.

"Winnie, girl, we know how much you love the ranch dogs, Milo and Lassie, and how much you were wishing for one of your own," he said, sending a smile to Christina.

In his arms was a tiny black ball of fur.

Winnie gasped and the little dog's head perked up. He gave a little yip of excitement as he spotted the girl. Waylon put the puppy on the floor and he ran straight to Winnie as though he knew how much the little girl already loved him. He wriggled into her arms and licked the dribbles of chocolate off Winnie's chin as she laughed.

"I love him, Daddy!" The puppy barked, as if he knew what she was saying. "Can we call him Mush? Like mushmellow?"

Waylon laughed. "We can name him whatever you like, sweetheart."

"Are you going to take him back to the base with you, Waylon?" his mother asked, curling the envelope Mr. Blade had given her in her hands. There were little smudges of moisture on the manila.

"Well, I was going to wait to tell you all, but I've decided not to reenlist. I have six more months, but then I'll be moving home. I was hoping to get a job—maybe with the sheriff's office, Wyatt?" He looked over at his brother.

Wyatt laughed. "Are you sure you want to come to work with me? You'd have to do real investigative work...and what did you call us? *Girl Scouts?*"

"What can I say?" Waylon said with a laugh. "I guess I'll start working on my merit badges."

Rainier glanced at their mother. The tears had returned and she sobbed into a tissue Merle had handed her. "Mom, are you going to be okay?"

She nodded.

Mr. Blade stepped back and gave Laura an awkward look, as though he wasn't sure if he should stay or go.

"Dad, here." Laura took him by the arm and had him sit on the couch next to her.

"I'm sorry..." Eloise said, trying to speak between sobs. "I'm just...so happy. I never thought this day would come."

"Then you may not want to open that envelope," Mr. Blade said.

All the laughter and voices in the room stopped. The only sound was of Mush as he hopped and crunched through the discarded wrapping paper around Winnie.

"No, it's not like that," Laura's dad said with a

wave. "Inside, you will find a great deal of paper-work."

"About what?" Merle asked.

"Basically, my team I have been talking. We met with the DA about your role in covering up Paul Poe's death. As it stands, and because of the amount of time that has gone by since the man's death, the DA doesn't wish to pursue any charges."

Eloise clapped her hands over her mouth. "Oh my… Thank you… Thank you so much."

"That's not all," Mr. Blade continued. "We also went through a great deal of records to do with your property as well as county tax records. We found that William Poe had pulled something similar to what he was trying to do with your family's ranch once before—after filing a lien against a family, he bought their property. That was the house where he and his late wife resided. With your records, and those from that sale, we were able to prove that he had the intention of doing the same with this property. Having that, along with the police report and what he said to you all, I talked to a judge and we made a filing against the Department of Revenue. Simply put, and providing there are no extenuating circumstances, your case is already won. You owe no additional taxes, and as soon as we have everything worked out and in order, I believe we have enough evidence for you to file a strong a lawsuit against the DR, should you wish to. In fact, I have it from a reliable source that they would be likely to settle in order to make things right with your family."

"What do you mean?" Eloise asked.

"I think we could get enough money that you and your family would never have to worry about losing the ranch ever again."

"Oh, Dad," Laura said. "Thank you so much."

Rainier stared at the scene around him. In all the nights he'd been surrounded by cinderblock walls and iron bars, he had never imagined a future that could be so magnificent. Though the world would undoubtedly bring the unexpected, he and Laura had the things in life that made it complete—love, family and a future brighter than even the brightest Christmas lights.

They would have one another forever.

* * * * *

Can't get enough of MYSTERY CHRISTMAS? *Check out the previous titles in the series:*

MS. CALCULATION
MR. SERIOUS
MR. TAKEN

Available now from Harlequin Intrigue!

*Sheriff Flint Cahill can and will endure elements
far worse than the coming winter storm to hunt
down Maggie Thompson and her abductor.*

Read on for a sneak preview of
COWBOY'S LEGACY,
A CAHILL RANCH NOVEL *from*
New York Times *bestselling author*
B.J. Daniels!

SHE WAS IN so fast that she didn't have a chance to scream. The icy cold water stole her breath away. Her eyes flew open as she hit. Because of the way she fell, she had no sense of up or down for a few moments.

Panicked, she flailed in the water until a light flickered above her. She tried to swim toward it, but something was holding her down. The harder she fought, the more it seemed to push her deeper and deeper, the light fading.

Her lungs burned. She had to breathe. The dim light wavered above her through the rippling water. She clawed at it as her breath gave out. She could see the surface just inches above her. Air! She needed oxygen. Now!

The rippling water distorted the face that suddenly appeared above her. The mouth twisted in a grotesque smile. She screamed, only to have her throat fill with the putrid dark water. She choked, sucking in even more water. She was drowning, and the person who'd done this to her was watching her die and smiling.

Maggie Thompson shot upright in bed, gasping for air and swinging her arms frantically toward the faint light coming through the window. Panic had her perspiration-soaked nightgown sticking to her skin. Trembling, she clutched the bedcovers as she gasped for breath.

The nightmare had been so real this time that she thought she was going to drown before she could come out of it. Her chest ached, her throat feeling raw as tears burned her eyes. It had been too real. She couldn't shake the feeling that she'd almost died this time. Next time…

She snapped on the bedside lamp to chase away the dark shadows hunkered in the corners of the room. If only Flint had been here instead of on an all-night stakeout. She needed Sheriff Flint Cahill's strong arms around her. Not that he stayed most nights. They hadn't been intimate that long.

Often, he had to work or was called out in the middle of the night. He'd asked her to move in with him months ago, but she'd declined. He'd asked her after one of his ex-wife's nasty tricks. Maggie hadn't wanted to make a decision like that based on Flint's ex.

While his ex hadn't done anything in months to

keep them apart, Maggie couldn't rest easy. Flint was hoping Celeste had grown tired of her tricks. Maggie wasn't that naive. Celeste Duma was one of those women who played on every man's weakness to get what she wanted—and she wanted not just the rich, powerful man she'd left Flint for. She wanted to keep her ex on the string, as well.

Maggie's breathing slowed a little. She pulled the covers up to her chin, still shivering, but she didn't turn off the light. Sleep was out of the question for a while. She told herself that she wasn't going to let Celeste scare her. She wasn't going to give the woman the satisfaction.

Unfortunately, it was just bravado. Flint's ex was obsessed with him. Obsessed with keeping them apart. And since the woman had nothing else to do…

As the images of the nightmare faded, she reminded herself that the dream made no sense. It never had. She was a good swimmer. Loved water. Had never nearly drowned. Nor had anyone ever tried to drown her.

Shuddering, she thought of the face she'd seen through the rippling water. Not Celeste's. More like a Halloween mask. A distorted smiling face, neither male nor female. Just the memory sent her heart racing again.

What bothered her most was that dream kept reoccurring. After the first time, she'd mentioned it to her friend Belle Delaney.

"A drowning dream?" Belle had asked with the arch of her eyebrow. "Do you feel that in waking life you're being 'sucked into' something you'd rather not be a part of?"

Maggie had groaned inwardly. Belle had never kept it a secret that she thought Maggie was making a mistake when it came to Flint. Too much baggage, she always said of the sheriff. His "baggage" came in the shape of his spoiled, probably psychopathic, petite, green-eyed, blonde ex.

"I have my own skeletons." Maggie had laughed, although she'd never shared her past—even with Belle—before moving to Gilt Edge, Montana, and opening her beauty shop, Just Hair. She feared it was her own baggage that scared her the most.

"If you're holding anything back," Belle had said, eyeing her closely, "you need to let it out. Men hate surprises after they tie the knot."

"Guess I don't have to worry about that because Flint hasn't said anything about marriage." But she knew Belle was right. She'd even come close to telling him several times about her past. Something had always stopped her. The truth was, she feared if he found out her reasons for coming to Gilt Edge he wouldn't want her anymore.

"The dream isn't about Flint," she'd argued that

day with Belle, but she couldn't shake the feeling that it was a warning.

"Well, from what I know about dreams," Belle had said, "if in the dream you survive the drowning, it means that a waking relationship will ultimately survive the turmoil. At least, that is one interpretation. But I'd say the nightmare definitely indicates that you are going into unknown waters and something is making you leery of where you're headed." She'd cocked an eyebrow at her. "If you have the dream again, I'd suggest that you ask yourself what it is you're so afraid of."

"I'm sure it's just about his ex, Celeste," she'd lied. Or was she afraid that she wasn't good enough for Flint—just as his ex had warned her. Just as she feared in her heart.

THE WIND LAY over the tall dried grass and kicked up dust as Sheriff Flint Cahill stood on the hillside. He shoved his Stetson down on his head of thick dark hair, squinting in the distance at the clouds to the west. Sure as the devil, it was going to snow before the day was out.

In the distance, he could see a large star made out of red and green lights on the side of a barn, a reminder that Christmas was coming. Flint thought he might even get a tree this year, go up in the mountains and cut it himself. He hadn't had a tree at Christmas in years. Not since…

At the sound of a pickup horn, he turned, shielding his eyes from the low winter sun. He could smell snow in the air, feel it deep in his bones. This storm was going to dump a good foot on them, according to the latest news. They were going to have a white Christmas.

Most years he wasn't ready for the holiday season any more than he was ready for a snow that wouldn't melt until spring. But this year was different. He felt energized. This was the year his life would change. He thought of the small velvet box in his jacket pocket. He'd been carrying it around for months. Just the thought of it made him smile to himself. He was in love and he was finally going to do something about it.

The pickup rumbled to a stop a few yards from him. He took a deep breath of the mountain air and, telling himself he was ready for whatever Mother Nature wanted to throw at him, he headed for the truck.

"Are you all right?" his sister asked as he slid into the passenger seat. In the cab out of the wind, it was nice and warm. He rubbed his bare hands together, wishing he hadn't forgotten his gloves earlier. But when he'd headed out, he'd had too much on his mind. He still did.

Lillie looked out at the dull brown of the landscape and the chain-link fence that surrounded the missile silo. "What were you doing out here?"

He chuckled. "Looking for aliens. What else?" This was the spot that their father swore aliens hadn't just landed on one night back in 1967. Nope, according to Ely Cahill, the aliens had abducted him, taken him aboard their spaceship and done experiments on him. Not that anyone believed it in the county. Everyone just assumed that Ely had a screw loose. Or two.

It didn't help that their father spent most of the year up in the mountains as a recluse trapping and panning for gold.

"Aliens. Funny," Lillie said, making a face at him.

He smiled over at her. "Actually, I was on an all-night stakeout. The cattle rustlers didn't show up." He shrugged.

She glanced around. "Where's your patrol SUV?"

"Axle deep in a muddy creek back toward Grass Range. I'll have to get it pulled out. After I called you, I started walking and I ended up here. Wish I'd grabbed my gloves, though."

"You're scaring me," she said, studying him openly. "You're starting to act like Dad."

He laughed at that, wondering how far from the truth it was. "At least I didn't see any aliens near the missile silo."

She groaned. Being the butt of jokes in the county because of their father got old for all of them.

Flint glanced at the fenced-in area. There was nothing visible behind the chain link but tumbleweeds. He turned back to her. "I didn't pull you away from anything important, I hope? Since you were close by, I thought you wouldn't mind giving me a ride. I've had enough walking for one day. Or thinking, for that matter."

She shook her head. "What's going on, Flint?"

He looked out at the country that ran to the mountains. Cahill Ranch. His grandfather had started it, his father had worked it and now two of his brothers ran the cattle part of it to keep the place going while he and his sister, Lillie, and brother Darby had taken other paths. Not to mention their oldest brother, Tucker, who'd struck out at seventeen and hadn't been seen or heard from since.

Flint had been scared after his marriage and divorce. But Maggie was nothing like Celeste, who was small, blonde, green-eyed and crazy. Maggie was tall with big brown eyes and long auburn hair. His heart beat faster at the thought of her smile, at her laugh.

"I'm going to ask Maggie to marry me," Flint said and nodded as if reassuring himself.

When Lillie didn't reply, he glanced over at her. It wasn't like her not to have something to say. "Well?"

"What has taken you so long?"

He sighed. "Well, you know after Celeste…"

"Say no more," his sister said, raising a hand to

stop him. "Anyone would be gun-shy after being married to her."

"I'm hoping she won't be a problem."

Lillie laughed. "Short of killing your ex-wife, she is always going to be a problem. You just have to decide if you're going to let her run your life. Or if you're going to live it—in spite of her."

So easy for her to say. He smiled, though. "You're right. Anyway, Maggie and I have been dating for a while now and there haven't been any…incidents in months."

Lillie shook her head. "You know Celeste was the one who vandalized Maggie's beauty shop—just as you know she started that fire at Maggie's house."

"Too bad there wasn't any proof so I could have arrested her. But since there wasn't and no one was hurt and it was months ago…"

"I'd love to see Celeste behind bars, though I think prison is too good for her. I can understand why you would be worried about what she will do next. She's psychopathic."

He feared that might be close to the case. "Do you want to see the ring?" He knew she did, so he fished it out of his pocket. He'd been carrying it around for quite a while now. Getting up his courage? He knew what was holding him back. Celeste. He couldn't be sure how she would take it—or what she might do. His ex-wife seemed determined that he and Maggie shouldn't be together, even though she was apparently happily married to local wealthy businessman Wayne Duma.

Handing his sister the small black velvet box, he waited as she slowly opened it.

A small gasp escaped her lips. "It's beautiful. *Really* beautiful." She shot him a look. "I thought sheriffs didn't make much money?"

"I've been saving for a long while now. Unlike my sister, I live pretty simply."

She laughed. "Simply? Prisoners have more in their cells than you do. You aren't thinking of living in that small house of yours after you're married, are you?"

"For a while. It's not that bad. Not all of us have huge new houses like you and Trask."

"We need the room for all the kids we're going to have," she said. "But it is wonderful, isn't it? Trask is determined that I have everything I ever wanted." Her gaze softened as the newlywed thought of her husband.

"I keep thinking of your wedding." There'd been a double wedding, with both Lillie and her twin, Darby, getting married to the loves of their lives only months ago. "It's great to see you and Trask so happy. And Darby and Mariah… I don't think Darby is ever going to come off that cloud he's on."

Lillie smiled. "I'm so happy for him. And I'm happy for you. You know I really like Maggie. So do it. Don't worry about Celeste. Once you're married, there's nothing she can do."

He told himself she was right, and yet in the back of his mind, he feared that his ex-wife would do something to ruin it—just as she had done to some of his dates with Maggie.

"I don't understand Celeste," Lillie was saying as she shifted into Drive and started toward the small Western town of Gilt Edge. "She's the one who dumped you for Wayne Duma. So what is her problem?"

"I'm worried that she is having second thoughts about her marriage to Duma. Or maybe she's bored and has nothing better to do than concern herself with my life. Maybe she just doesn't want me to be happy."

"Or she is just plain malicious," Lillie said. "If she isn't happy, she doesn't want you to be, either."

A shaft of sunlight came through the cab window, warming him against the chill that came with even talking about Celeste. He leaned back, content as Lillie drove.

He was going to ask Maggie to marry him. He was going to do it this weekend. He'd already made a dinner reservation at the local steak house. He had the ring in his pocket. Now it was just a matter of popping the question and hoping she said yes. If she did… Well, then, this was going to be the best Christmas ever, he thought and smiled.

* * * * *

Don't miss COWBOY'S LEGACY,
available December 2017
wherever HQN Books and ebooks are sold.

www.Harlequin.com

COMING NEXT MONTH FROM

H HARLEQUIN®

INTRIGUE

Available December 19, 2017

#1755 GUNFIRE ON THE RANCH
Blue River Ranch • by Delores Fossen
DEA agent Theo Carter was a suspect in his parents' murder...and now he's back to protect the family he never knew he had.

#1756 SAFE AT HAWK'S LANDING
Badge of Justice • by Rita Herron
Charlotte Reacher is no stranger to the trauma her students have experienced, and as she's the only witness to a human-trafficking abduction, FBI agent Lucas Hawk will have his work cut out for him keeping her safe.

#1757 WHISPERING SPRINGS
by Amanda Stevens
This high school reunion was a shot at redemption and maybe a second chance for former army ranger Dylan Burkhart and his old flame Ava North. But a secret-telling game turns up a murder confession, with the killer hiding among them...

#1758 RANGER PROTECTOR
Texas Brothers of Company B • by Angi Morgan
After Megan Harper is framed for a fatal shooting, protecting her becomes Texas Ranger Jack McKinnon's sole mission...until unspoken desire gets in the way.

#1759 SOLDIER'S PROMISE
The Ranger Brigade: Family Secrets • by Cindi Myers
Different circumstances brought officer Jake Lohmiller and undercover Ranger Brigade sergeant Carmen Redhorse to a cult encampment in Colorado, but teaming up might be their only shot at saving their families... and each other.

#1760 FORGOTTEN PIECES
The Protectors of Riker County • by Tyler Anne Snell
To say Riker County detective Matt Walker and journalist Maggie Carson have bad blood is an understatement. But when the last twenty-four hours of her memory go missing and she gets caught in someone's crosshairs, the lawman who hates her may be her only salvation...

HICNM1217

Get 2 Free Books,
Plus 2 Free Gifts—
just for trying the
Reader Service!

SPECIAL EXCERPT FROM

⧫HHARLEQUIN®

I N T R I G U E

*To say Riker County detective Matt Walker and
journalist Maggie Carson have bad blood is an
understatement. But when the last twenty-four hours
of her memory go missing and she gets caught in
someone's crosshairs, the lawman who hates her may be
her only salvation...*

Read on for a sneak preview of
FORGOTTEN PIECES
by Tyler Anne Snell.

Everyone worked through grief differently.

Some people started a new hobby; some people threw themselves into the gym.

Others investigated unsolved murders in secret.

"And why, of all people, would you need me here?" Matt asked, cutting through her mental breakdown of him.

Instead of stepping backward, utilizing the large open space of her front porch, she chanced a step forward.

"I found something," she started, straining out any excess enthusiasm that might make her seem coarse. Still, she knew the detective was a keen observer. Which was why his frown was already doubling in on itself before she explained herself.

"I don't want to hear this," he interrupted, his voice like ice. "I'm warning you, Carson."

"And it wouldn't be the first time you've done so," she countered, skipping over the fact he'd said her last name like a teacher getting ready to send her to detention. "But right now I'm telling you I found a lead. A real, honest-to-God lead!"

The detective's frown affected all of his body. It pinched his expression and pulled his posture taut. Through gritted teeth, he rumbled out his thoughts with disdain clear in his words.

"Why do you keep doing this? What gives you the right?" He took a step away from her. That didn't stop Maggie.

"It wasn't an accident," she implored. "I can prove it now."

Matt shook his head. He skipped frustrated and flew right into angry. This time Maggie faltered.

"You have no right digging into this," he growled. "You didn't even know Erin."

"But don't you want to hear what I found?"

Matt made a stop motion with his hands. The jaw she'd been admiring was set. Hard. "I don't want to ever talk to you again. Especially about this." He turned and was off the front porch in one fluid motion. Before he got into his truck he paused. "And next time you call me out here, I won't hesitate to arrest you."

And then he was gone.

Don't miss
FORGOTTEN PIECES
available January 2018 wherever
Harlequin® Intrigue books and ebooks are sold.

www.Harlequin.com

HIEXP1217